Silver Spurs

Horses and Friends Series

A Horse for Kate
Silver Spurs
Mystery Rider (Fall 2015)
Blue Ribbon Trail Ride (Spring 2016)

MIRALEE FERRELL

SilverSpurs

David C Cook

transforming lives together

SILVER SPURS
Published by David C Cook
4050 Lee Vance View
Colorado Springs, CO 80918 U.S.A.

David C Cook Distribution Canada
55 Woodslee Avenue, Paris, Ontario, Canada N3L 3E5

David C Cook U.K., Kingsway Communications
Eastbourne, East Sussex BN23 6NT, England

The graphic circle C logo is a registered trademark of David C Cook.

LCCN 2014957983
ISBN 978-0-7814-1113-4
eISBN 978-1-4347-0928-8

© 2015 Miralee Ferrell
Published in association with Tamela Hancock Murray of The Steve
Laube Agency, 5025 N. Central Ave., #635, Phoenix, AZ 85012

The Team: Ingrid Beck, Ramona Cramer Tucker, Nick Lee,
Amy Konyndyk, Tiffany Thomas, Karen Athen
Cover Design: DogEared Design, Kirk DouPonce

Printed in the United States of America
First Edition 2015

3 4 5 6 7 8 9 10 11 12 13

031616

To Kate, my darling granddaughter.
I hope by the time you're old enough
to read these books, you'll love horses
and reading as much as I do.

Chapter One

Upper Hood River Valley, Odell, Oregon
May, Present Day

Kate Ferris hauled back on the reins and brought her Thoroughbred mare to a stop. Her arms ached with the effort. Capri was a lot of horse to keep under control.

The mare tossed her head, and froth flew from her mouth.

Kate patted the mare's neck, her palms sweaty against the dark-red coat. "Easy, girl. Settle down. It's okay." *It's really not okay.* Kate frowned, hoping her voice didn't show her frustration. Determination pushed her forward. No way could she quit and let Capri win this battle. Kate hadn't learned as much as she'd liked in the few lessons she'd taken while working at the English-riding barn a couple of miles from home, but she knew she shouldn't reward Capri by dismounting when the mare wasn't responding to her cues.

The chestnut horse threw her head again and pranced in place.

Kate gave an exasperated sigh. "All right, let's try it again. Slower this time." She nudged her mount into a trot along the rail of the outdoor arena, trying to focus on rising and falling to the beat of the Thoroughbred's long stride. Getting the hang of posting hadn't been easy, but Kate finally had it mastered. At least she *hoped* she'd mastered it.

Capri pricked her ears, broke into a canter, and ducked her head, throwing Kate off balance. Kate scrambled to stay in her seat, clutching Capri's mane for a moment before gripping the mare's sides hard with her knees. She planted her feet more firmly in the stirrup irons and pulled her horse to a standstill. "I give up." Her shoulders hunched in defeat.

She had been *so* excited when God brought Capri into her life. Her dream of owning a horse had finally come true! Kate believed it wouldn't be long before she could compete in shows around their area—maybe even qualify for the regional championships in the fall. She'd never expected to own a mare who'd had professional hunter-jumper training.

Problem was, Capri had stood in a pasture for over a year when her owner got sick, with no one to help her maintain what she'd learned. During the past several weeks, Kate's hopes had crashed as she came face-to-face with her own poor horsemanship.

Capri was well trained and smart—maybe too smart. She took advantage of the tiniest bit of hesitation on Kate's part, making it obvious the horse had a mind of her own. She was smart enough to figure out she had a novice in the saddle.

Running the palm of her hand along the mare's sweaty neck, Kate loosened her grip on the reins and urged Capri toward the gate. She leaned over and pushed it open, then rode toward the barn where her mother was working. "Mom! I need you."

Nan Ferris hurried from the open doorway, dusting bits of hay off her jeans. "What is it? I'm trying to organize the tack room."

"I can't do this anymore." Kate lifted her chin, her frustration at Capri bubbling to the surface. She bit her lip to keep it from trembling.

"Do what?" Her mother's hazel eyes narrowed as she stared at the sweating mare. "Have you been running that horse?"

"No. I've been working her in the arena, but I don't know enough, Mom. I'll never get her ready for a show at this rate."

Her mother sighed. "We've discussed this, Kate. You're taking lessons once a week in exchange for cleaning stalls. Your father and I can't afford more right now. Honey ... why can't you be thankful you have a horse to love and ride, and not worry about showing?"

Kate swallowed the irritation pressing to escape. Mom didn't understand how important it was to her to learn to ride better. Sure, she knew the basics, but she'd dreamed of competing ever since her aunt took her to a horse show a couple of years ago. It wasn't like Kate spent a lot of money on clothes. All she'd ever wanted was a horse, but now that she had one, she longed to learn more.

"I've barely started riding a full-size horse instead of Lulu. I love it, but I only have an hour lesson a week. It's not enough, and they aren't teaching me to jump."

Kate heard the complaining in her voice and winced. She knew her dad was working hard to pay for their recent move and to make up for being without a job for so long. With her little brother Peter's autism, and his need for after-school care, her mother had her hands full.

When her mom didn't say anything, Kate swung off her horse and pulled the reins over her mare's head. "I'll walk Capri for a bit and cool her down, then I'll help with the barn." She kicked a dirt clod. "Mom?"

"Yes?"

Kate placed her palm against Capri's neck and grinned. She had the perfect plan ... if only Mom would agree. "We have a lot of empty stalls. Can't we advertise and take in boarders? I could clean stalls and feed the horses. And earn money for lessons."

Her mother paused at the big rollaway doors. "Your dad and I considered tearing down this indoor arena or converting it into a storage building. Your grandfather used to board horses here when I was growing up, but his accident is one of the reasons I quit riding. Mother was terrified I'd get hurt too."

"I know, Mom. I've heard that story a million times." Kate bit the inside of her cheek and closed her eyes. Why couldn't Mom understand how important this was? It wasn't like they had miles of trails close by where she could ride, since her parents didn't want her riding alone away from the barn. It was boring walking or trotting Capri around in the arena without knowing how to use Capri's training.

She worked to calm her voice. "I'm sorry. It's just that I want this so bad. Would you at least talk to Dad about it? Please?" Her heart raced. "We could have our own business. Maybe even get a professional trainer to give lessons, and we could host shows."

Her mother narrowed her eyes. "Not so fast, young lady. There's a lot to think about. We'd have to check with our insurance agent and see what coverage would cost. The arena needs work, and it means putting out money for hay, shavings, and additional feed. I'll admit it has potential, but it has to work financially. I'll talk to your father when he gets home, if he's not too tired."

"It'll work. I know it will." Kate tugged at her mare's reins. "Come on, Capri. I'm going to make this place shine ... after I clean your stall, that is." She shot her mother a look. Mom did a lot around the place, as well as working part-time from their home and caring for Pete. Somehow Kate had to prove she could pull her own weight. "And feed the rabbits and take Rufus for a walk."

A loud bark behind her made Kate jump. She swung around in time to see her ninety-pound German shepherd launch himself across the grass toward her. Capri danced at the end of her reins as the large dog drew closer. Kate held up her hand. "Rufus! Sit, boy!"

Rufus stopped a few inches from Kate's toes. His tongue hung out, and he turned adoring eyes up to meet hers. Then he plopped down and extended a paw.

Kate giggled and dug into her pocket, withdrawing a treat and dropping it into his eager mouth. "Good boy. Did you see that, Mom? I've been working with him, and he finally got it."

Her mother's eyebrows disappeared under her bangs. "Amazing. He's never done that before."

"He's smart." Kate ruffled the fur on his head and scratched behind his ears. "Aren't you, buddy?"

Rufus woofed a reply. Kate could have sworn he was grinning.

"Come on, Rufus. Let's put Capri in her stall." Kate hesitated. "So ... when will you call the insurance agent? Like right now, maybe?"

A tiny smile tugged at the corners of her mom's mouth. "We'll see what your dad has to say first."

"Can I call Tori? She'll be *so* excited." The reminder of her best friend sent Kate's spirits soaring. Tori loved hanging out at their barn.

"You can talk to Tori, but I'm not making any promises. Even if Dad agrees, there's a lot of work to do before this can happen." She hugged Kate. "I know you're excited, honey, but please don't get your hopes up." Her mother's smile faded.

"Why? What's wrong?"

Her mother sucked in a sharp breath and blew it out slowly. "I'm not sure how your brother will fit into this. It's not like Pete can do anything with horses."

"Aw, Mom!" Kate clenched her fists. Why did Pete always have to come first? Couldn't anything be for *her*? This *had* to work. Tori would be in heaven if Kate's family had a riding stable. Tori didn't have a horse, and her family couldn't afford to buy one.

We could ride horses together, and take lessons, and … Kate's thoughts whirled.

Then reality hit. She gritted her teeth. *Or not!* "That's not fair, Mom! Pete can sit out here and watch while we work. He doesn't have to stay in the house. We shouldn't baby him just because he has autism."

"I'm not trying to, Kate." Mom smiled. "You pray about it, and so will I. Besides, we don't even know if anyone would want to board their horses here."

Kate tried to force herself to relax. She wrapped Capri's reins around a fence rail, then turned to face her mother. "Sure they will. Tons of people around here own horses. Besides, I've heard about riding programs for special-needs kids. Maybe we could find an instructor who would work with Pete. That could bring in even more business, as well as being good for him." Hope surged through her. "We're in some of the best horse country in the Columbia River Gorge, if not the entire Northwest. There are only two show barns in all of the Upper Hood River Valley and none in The Dalles or across the river in White Salmon."

"Sounds like you've been thinking about this for a while." Her mother tucked a curly wisp of hair behind Kate's ear. "I'll find out what the other barns charge and ask if they're full. Go take care of your horse. Pete's taking a nap, but I'd better check on him."

Kate gazed after her mother as she walked along the path to their two-story house set back in the trees. She loved her six-year-old brother with all her heart, but she hoped he wouldn't be the cause of them not getting to run a boarding stable.

She slapped the riding crop against her leg. Somehow she'd find a way to make this work. Mom spent so much time caring for Pete that Kate often felt left out. Couldn't it be her turn to have something *she* wanted for a change?

The suggestion to pray about the new project flitted through Kate's mind, but she pushed it away. She loved God, but sometimes He didn't seem very practical. After all, He hadn't kept Pete from being disabled, and He hadn't answered her prayers for more money to help her parents pay the bills. Why should she think He'd care about her dream of owning a show barn and taking lessons?

An instant later, shame washed over her as she was reminded of the miracle of Capri's arrival. God had done that, no mistake. "All right," she whispered heavenward. "Maybe You could help on this request too, if it's not too much to ask?"

Chapter Two

Kate twisted her hair around her finger and leaned back in the worn-out lawn chair parked outside the barn door. "I'm tired. I didn't know this place needed so much work. We've done a lot this past week, and we're still not done."

Tori took a drink of her soda. "I'm thankful we had Colt's help, or it never would have gotten done." She peered at the boy tipped back in the lounge chair with his eyes closed. They'd met him shortly after Kate arrived in town, but he was already becoming a good friend. "It started out dirty, but it's getting better." She pointed at Kate's face and smirked. "I think you got most of the dirt on your face. And your brown hair looks gray with the dust and cobwebs all over it."

"Gross!" Kate sat up and batted at her hair. She hated spiders more than anything! Snakes she could deal with, but those eight-legged little creatures gave her the creeps.

Tori choked back a laugh. "Sorry, I was teasing about the cobwebs. But your hair *is* gray."

Kate flopped against the chair and groaned. "Thanks a lot. At least I don't have straw in my hair and mud on my nose." She grinned, knowing how much Tori disliked looking grubby.

Teasing her best friend took Kate's mind off her sore feet and aching back. Besides, Tori always got even, as she'd proved with her crack about the cobwebs. "I guess we should water Capri and toss her some feed now that the stalls are clean."

Soft footfalls sounded behind her, and Kate turned. "Pete. What's up? Want to sit with me, Colt, and Tori?"

Colt sat up and smiled at Kate's little brother. "You can sit with me, buddy."

Pete scuffled one foot back and forth, back and forth, his brown head bowed.

Tori glanced at Kate, then sat up slowly, swinging her legs over the edge of the lounger and scooting over, resting her shoulder against the raised back of the chair. "Hey, kiddo. I have half a package of M&M's left. Want some?" She dug into her pocket and took out a crumpled packet.

Pete shrugged but shifted his feet a few inches her direction.

She patted the seat beside her. "Come on. There's plenty of room. I saved you all the red ones."

His eyes flitted up, and then his gaze darted away, but he sidled closer until he was within reach.

Kate smiled, relieved that her little brother was responding so well to Tori. Her friend wanted to work with disabled kids when she grew up, and she'd connected with Pete from the moment she met him. Kate loved Pete more than almost anyone in her life, but it was hard to imagine having the patience to spend hours with a roomful of people who needed so much help. That made her friend even more special.

Kate leaned toward Colt. "Don't feel bad. He doesn't know you very well yet, and Tori's his favorite right now. Especially since she has M&M's."

Pete sank slowly onto the lounger next to Tori but still didn't meet her gaze. He held out his hand and waited as she tumbled a pile of M&M's onto his palm. "Thank you." The simple words were low and soft.

Tori's face lit up in response. "You're welcome. Hey, do you want to see what we've been doing in the barn?"

He shook his head and hunched into a ball. "Just want candy."

"Okay, that's cool. You can sit with us as long as you want."

Colt pushed to his feet and stretched. "I'd better get going. I still have homework to do, and Mom told me I had to get it done before tonight, since we've got a superbusy day tomorrow."

Kate looked up at the boy who was taller than she was, something that didn't happen a lot at her age, since she was taller than most of the boys in her seventh-grade class. "Thanks, Colt. You've been awesome. We couldn't have done this without you and Tori."

Pete eased out of Tori's chair. "Going to the house now. M&M's are all gone." He held up his hands but still didn't meet anyone's eyes.

Colt grinned. "I'll walk him to the house, since my bike is parked by your door. See you guys later."

"Bye, Colt." Tori waved. "I'll bring more candy next time I come, Pete."

Pete didn't reply, but Kate was sure she saw a tiny smile play at the corners of his mouth. "You're so good with him. Once we have a trainer and learn more, maybe we can teach Pete to ride."

The smile eased off Tori's face, and she sighed. "At least you and Colt each have a horse to take lessons on when you hire an instructor."

Kate sat up with a jerk. "*If* we get an instructor. Mom and Dad haven't decided yet."

"Well, they said yes to thinking about taking horses to board. And you'll be able to use Capri for lessons."

"Hey, you're my best friend. I'm not going to leave you out."

"Not like you have much choice. I'll never get a horse." Tori scrunched her brows. "I can be your groom."

The muscles in Kate's stomach tightened. Tori became her best friend not long after Kate and her family moved to Odell in March. She hated hearing the hurt in Tori's voice. "No way." Kate jumped from the chair, knocking it onto its side. "Come on."

"What?" Tori sat still and stared up at her. "I've done enough work today. I want to drink my pop."

Kate giggled and reached for Tori's hand, excitement surging through her. "Get out of that chair. Hurry up." She pulled Tori to her feet. "I've got a plan, and you're going to love it."

Tori swung into step with Kate. "What's up?"

"You'll see. Help me tack up Capri."

"Huh?" Tori put on the brakes. "You rode her before I came."

Kate swung around, allowing a grin to spread across her face. She couldn't wait to see Tori's reaction. "I know. Stop with all the questions and help me, all right?"

Tori shuffled forward. "Okay, okay. You're awful bossy."

"You'll be glad in a few minutes." Kate reached for the royal-blue halter and matching rope hanging on a horseshoe hook next to the stall door. She slid the door open, then slipped a carrot out of her jeans pocket and handed it to her snuffling mare, who always seemed to know when treats were near. "There you go. You'll get more later, girl."

Tori jogged to the tack room, brought back the box of brushes, and set them down. She made another trip, returning with the saddle and pad. "When are you gonna tell me what you're up to?"

Kate rushed through grooming her horse, then tossed the brush into the box and swung the saddle pad onto Capri's back, ignoring her friend's question. *Tori'll love this. I just know it!* "Grab her bridle with the snaffle bit and a lunge line. Oh, and my helmet."

"Sure thing, *boss*." Tori shot her a mystified look and disappeared into the tack room again. She came back with the helmet, bridle, and lunge line clutched in her hands. She set the helmet on top of the grooming tools and waited till Kate cinched the saddle and reached for the bridle. "Enough already. Spill."

Kate grinned. "You're going to ride Capri too. I'm sharing her with you!" Why hadn't she thought of this before? Her friend wanted a horse in the worst way, and she was right. Her parents couldn't afford one. Best friends were supposed to share everything—secrets, dreams, clothes. So why not a horse?

Tori backed up a step. "No way. I'm a beginner, and she's a lot of horse."

Kate dangled the coiled, thirty-foot lunge line with confidence. "That's what this is for, silly. I'm not going to turn you loose on my horse. We'll walk her around in a circle today so you can get used to her. By the time we have a trainer and boarders wanting lessons, you'll be ready."

"I don't know. I haven't ridden much."

"Just put the helmet on and quit worrying." Kate grabbed the black helmet and shoved it into Tori's hands. "Breeches would be better, since they're more comfortable, and I wish we had English chaps so the stirrup leathers won't pinch your calves, but your boots and jeans will work. Besides, you won't be riding long enough or fast enough to be bothered. I think you're set."

Kate slipped the bit into Capri's mouth and slid the headstall over her ears. After securing the straps, Kate snapped the lunge line to the circular bit ring. "Come on." She led her mare into the arena and stopped her next to a mounting block. Capri stood with her head down, apparently not too excited about her second ride of the day. "Use this to step up on. You won't pull the saddle off that way."

Tori walked up the three-step mounting block, then paused. "Do you want me to hold the reins?"

"Sure, but not very tight. Go on. Swing up."

Her friend did as she was told and settled gingerly into the saddle. She picked up the reins, pushed her feet into the iron stirrups, and smiled. "This isn't so bad. But you know I've only been taking lessons on Lulu at the other barn, and Capri is a lot taller than a pony."

Kate laughed. "Yeah. Capri is over sixteen hands. You ready?" Her excitement built. This was one of the best ideas she'd had in a long time. They could share Capri when they took lessons, and Tori wouldn't feel left out all the time.

"I guess."

"You'll be fine." Kate moved to the inside of the arena and clucked. Capri walked forward, ears flicking and tail swishing. This was easy. Pride swelled in Kate's heart. She'd made the right decision sharing with Tori. There was nothing to being a trainer or giving lessons to a beginner. As long as Capri was secured with a lunge line, nothing could happen.

The mare walked at a sedate pace around the perimeter two times, and Kate made a decision. Tori sat comfortably and seemed to be enjoying herself. "I'm going to ask her to trot."

"No! I don't want to. I've only ridden Lulu a few times, and she's short and feels different." Tori grabbed the front of the English saddle as Capri moved into a faster gait. Tori's body bounced with the horse's motion, and her legs slapped the saddle fenders. "Stop her, Kate."

"Whoa." Kate yanked the line and stepped toward her mare, but Capri didn't listen. She snorted, shook her head, and picked up her pace, settling into a canter.

"Kate!" Tori's voice rose to a shriek, and she leaned over the mare's neck, gripping her mane. "I want off *right now*."

Fear shot through Kate. "Pull back on the reins." She walked a couple of feet closer to the center of the circle. "Capri. Whoa, girl. Easy." The horse skittered sideways away from Kate, giving a hop-skip as Kate edged closer.

Tori's inside foot bounced out of the stirrup, and her other foot continued to slap the mare's side. "I'm falling!"

"Hold on to her mane, Tori. Grip with your legs and hold on. I'll stop her." Kate tugged hard on the lunge line, praying Capri would listen.

Tori tipped to the side, and Kate watched in horror as her friend slid off the horse and onto the ground. "Tori!" She dropped the line and ran toward the center of the arena. Her heart slammed against the inside of her chest. "Are you hurt?"

Kate's stomach lurched when her friend didn't answer. The dirt was deep there. Tori couldn't be hurt—she just couldn't be! But why wasn't she getting up? Capri slowed and stopped halfway down the arena by the rail, her head hanging and the reins dangling. The mare was seemingly content to do nothing now that she'd unloaded her rider.

Kate skidded to a halt next to Tori, her hands shaking. Tori lay on the ground with her eyes closed. Suddenly she coughed. "Can't breathe."

"I'll get Mom. Don't move." Kate raced across the arena and headed for the house. Her best friend couldn't be seriously hurt. It would be all her fault if she was. Kate almost stopped running, but there was no time now to reflect on what Mom or Dad would say. *Why didn't I think things through before I did something so foolish?*

A minute later, Kate flew across the arena with her mother on her heels. Mom was always telling Kate she was too impulsive. Kate knew Capri acted up sometimes, but she'd been so sure that the mare would behave herself on the lunge line. She'd envisioned herself as a trainer—stupid, that's what she was.

"Tori, are you alive?" She bent over Tori and peered into her friend's eyes. At least they were open now. That was a good sign. "Can you talk?"

"I guess so." Tori drew in a hard breath and coughed again.

Mom knelt and smoothed Tori's hair off her forehead. "Where does it hurt, honey?"

"All over."

Kate tried to hold back the tears. "Can you move your legs?"

Tori shifted her position on the ground and rotated her ankles, then bent her knees. "My legs are okay, I guess."

Mom blew a strand of hair out of her eyes before turning to Kate. "*What in the world* happened here? Why was Tori riding Capri?"

"It was my idea, Mom. I made her do it. I'm so sorry." Tears brimmed over Kate's lower eyelashes and trickled down her face, but she didn't care. She'd been brain-dead to think she could give Tori lessons.

Tori pushed up on one elbow. "No, you didn't. I wanted to."

Kate would have loved nothing more than to believe that, but she had to be honest, especially after the way she'd acted. "Nuh-uh." She shook her head. "You said she looked too big, and you were scared, but I didn't listen. I didn't mean for you to get hurt. You don't hate me, do you?"

"Of course not. You're my best friend. I'd never hate you. Now help me up."

Mom placed her arm under Tori's shoulders and helped her sit. "Are you sure? How are you feeling?"

"A lot better. I think hitting the ground knocked the wind out of my lungs. I don't hurt anywhere now." She reached her hand toward Kate. "Come on. Pull me up."

Relief flooded Kate, and she grinned. "Cool. Then I guess we should catch Capri and unsaddle her."

"No, young lady." Mom glared up at Kate. "*You'll* catch Capri and unsaddle her, not Tori. She needs to rest. Better yet, I'll drive her home. She could have been seriously injured. No more letting anyone ride your horse without checking with me first. Understood?"

"Yes, Mom." Kate kicked at a clod of dirt. The relief she'd felt evaporated. Tori said she felt fine, but dread wormed its way into Kate's mind. What if this accident had crippled her friend? Kate suddenly felt sick. "Are you sure you're okay?" she whispered to Tori.

Tori scowled. "Knock it off. I'm fine." She glanced at Kate's mother. "Mrs. Ferris, I appreciate you wanting to take me home, but I'm really okay."

Kate stared at her friend for another long moment, wanting to be sure. At the stubborn little tilt of Tori's chin, Kate's tense shoulders relaxed. "Good." She swung toward her mom. "This is why we need a trainer. It wouldn't have happened if we had someone at our barn giving us real lessons instead of me trying to teach Tori."

Mom rose to her feet. "This wouldn't have happened if you'd asked me if it was all right for Tori to ride Capri. I'd have said no or told you I had to be there to help. You can't make these decisions on your own, Kate." She planted her hands on her hips. "Accidents like this can get a barn closed down and make insurance rates go through the roof, not to mention risking the life of a novice rider. Promise me you'll never do something like this again."

"I'm sorry, Mom." Kate scuffed her toe in the dirt. "But you don't have to get so mad."

Tori dusted off her pants, then leaned over to whisper near Kate's ear. "Your mom's right. She might not let us board horses if you keep arguing."

"I didn't think of that," Kate mumbled low enough so her mother couldn't hear. She heaved a sigh, knowing she'd been wrong. "I'm *really* sorry, Mom. I'll take care of Capri while you drive Tori home."

"Good decision." Her mother tapped each girl's head in turn. "You gave me a scare. I love you both, and I don't want anything to happen to either of you." She wrapped an arm around Tori and drew her close. "Let's take you home and talk to your mom about riding lessons—and more than just a half hour or an hour a week."

"Huh?" Tori raised wide eyes.

"I think it's time we see about getting a trainer and opening this barn for business. If you girls are determined to ride, you need to learn the safe way to do so." She turned to Kate and smiled. "Your dad and I discussed it, and we've decided to turn this into a boarding stable if the two of you are willing to help."

"Yippee!" Kate shrieked and jumped a foot off the ground. "Colt will too, Mom!" She grabbed Tori's hands and drew her into a hug. "We're going to have a real barn. Isn't that the best thing you've ever heard?"

Tori's eyes shone. "Totally. Thanks, Mrs. Ferris. I'll help any way I can."

Kate's mom patted Tori's back. "I appreciate that. Kate will need to muck stalls and feed the horses, but it shouldn't take more than an hour or so after school—pretty much like you've been doing at the other barn. That is, if your mother will allow you to help, Tori. Kate and I can feed the horses in the mornings, but Kate, it means getting up earlier than you're used to."

Kate hugged herself with joy. "That's okay, I don't mind. I bet Colt would want to bring his horse here, if he can work off part of his board. Can we put an ad in the paper tomorrow, Mom?"

Kate wanted to dance around the arena. Once she took some lessons, she might even get to compete in a show. *If I win, maybe Mom and Dad will even notice me more.* A twinge of guilt tugged at her. It wasn't that they ignored her, but Pete took so much of Mom's time, and Dad worked a lot of hours at his job.

"Not so fast, young lady. We still have more cleanup to do and shavings and hay to order. Dad and I figured we can start advertising next week. Hopefully we'll get some boarders soon, since the other barns are pretty full. And after this stunt, your dad and I will have a few extra chores for you as well."

Kate hung her head for a moment. "Yeah, okay." Then it hit her again. Mom had said yes about the barn! She pivoted toward her friend, a hundred ideas bouncing around. "I can't wait! It's going to be so much fun, huh, Tori?"

"Yeah. Only one thing worries me."

"What's that?" Kate couldn't imagine anything going wrong now. They'd have a trainer and lessons in no time.

"I heard a couple of the girls in the equestrian club talking about the barns getting full and not having enough room for their horses. They're so snooty. They have a list of rules on how everything is supposed to be done. I hope none of those girls bring their horses here."

"Nah. They're all in a group across the valley. You wait and see. We'll only get nice kids at our barn." A little warning bell went off in Kate's mind, but she pushed it away. Nothing would rob her of the joy of operating a boarding stable. She knew it was going to be perfect.

Chapter Three

Two weeks after Tori's fall, Kate linked her arm with her friend's, her cheeks stretched tight from a happy grin. They gazed across the paddock area where a horse backed out of a trailer.

"Can you believe it's finally happening?" She squeezed Tori's arm and whispered, not wanting the new boarder to hear.

Tori's head bobbed in agreement. "I know. We got the barn all cleaned, and people are answering your mom's ad. It's so cool!"

"Yeah, and Dad even gave up his time off on Saturday to paint the tack room and put up new shelves." She heaved a satisfied sigh. "Mom says we have two more horses coming tomorrow."

"Do you know who they belong to?"

Kate shrugged. "I was so excited that I didn't think about asking. My parents said if we get at least four students, it'll be enough to talk to a trainer about lessons. Plus, Colt said he'd move his horse over too, and do chores for part of his board."

She tugged Tori forward as the horse disappeared into the barn. "Isn't that gelding beautiful?"

"Yeah. He's a Thoroughbred, right?"

Kate eyed the horse, noting the long, lean body and the prominent withers. "Yeah. I'll bet he's almost seventeen hands, 'cause he looks taller than Capri."

Tori gave a visible shudder. "I'd hate to fall off *him*. It was far enough to the ground on Capri."

Kate bit her lip. She still felt like a jerk for forcing her friend to ride when she knew Tori was scared. "I'm sorry you got hurt."

Tori elbowed her in the side. "You've said that, like, a hundred times now, so stop it. It's not like you pushed me off your horse."

Kate smiled. Why couldn't everyone be as understanding as Tori? This past week Kate had had a run-in with a couple of girls at school. She still smarted over a remark one of them—Melissa Tolbert—had made. Melissa had been the snottiest to Kate since she'd moved to Odell in March. "Okay. Come on. Let's introduce ourselves and find out the horse's name. I'm not sure if the man who walked him in is the owner or just the person who drove the truck."

"I heard a car drive up and park on the other side of the barn a couple of minutes ago." Tori pointed toward the gravel parking area outside the big sliding doors. "It could be the owners."

A door opened on the side of the barn, and Kate's mom poked her head out. "Kate! Can you and Tori come here? I'd like you to show our new boarder where to put her horse while her mother fills out the forms."

"Sure, Mom." Kate beckoned to Tori. "Come on. Maybe they'll let us groom their horse if they can't come every day."

"That would be awesome." Tori slipped through the open door ahead of Kate, then skidded to a halt. "What's *she* doing here?"

"Who?" Kate stepped up beside Tori and looked where she pointed. Kate's jaw dropped, and she quickly covered her mouth to keep from saying something she shouldn't.

She couldn't believe who was holding the gelding's lead rope—Melissa Tolbert. The girl who regularly dissed Kate … and had gone out of her way to do the same thing to Tori after Tori befriended Kate.

At that moment, Melissa's eyes met Kate's, and they widened. Melissa swiveled toward a tall brunette woman who looked as if she could have been Melissa's older sister. "Mom, this isn't a good idea."

Kate opened her mouth, wanting nothing more than to put the girl in her place, then snapped it shut and gritted her teeth. This was a customer. A rude one, but still a customer. Right now they needed all the business they could get. She mustered a smile. "Hey, Melissa. Nice horse." It sounded lame even to her, but it was all she could force out.

"Hmmph." Melissa's dark-blonde curls bounced on her shoulders as she swung away from Kate. "Mom, are you sure this is the only barn with an opening? I don't want to leave Mocha with"—she flipped the end of the rope toward Kate and Tori and scowled—"inexperienced people. They might not know how to take proper care of a Thoroughbred."

Mrs. Tolbert cast a look at Kate's mom, who stared at Melissa. Mrs. Tolbert inclined her head. "Forgive my daughter. She's disappointed she can't board her mare where most of the Pony Club members board their horses, and the owners are very exacting in their care and meet the members' expectations."

Melissa spun on her heel and frowned. "It's not necessary for you to apologize for me, Mom." She waved her hand around, then turned toward Kate's mom. "I suppose we don't have a lot of choice right now, but I do hope you'll do everything the same way the members of our Pony Club have been taught."

Melissa's mom gave her a tolerant smile. "There might be an opening at another facility in a couple of months, but we'll make do here for now." She turned to Kate's mom. "You *will* have a quality trainer coming in to give lessons, won't you? I'd hate to have to trailer Mocha across town."

Mom nodded. "I've contacted a trainer with excellent references. She'll give group lessons if we have a minimum of four students. We have three now, and your daughter makes four. I'm sure it won't be long before we'll have more. I'm curious, why didn't you stay at the barn where you were boarding?"

Kate held her breath, half hoping Melissa's mom would decide their barn wasn't good enough for her daughter's horse and leave. A prick of conscience niggled at Kate. They'd done a lot of work getting the barn ready, and her parents had spent money they probably couldn't afford. She'd best be asking God to let Melissa stay, not leave, no matter how much Kate would hate having her here.

Mrs. Tolbert's smile faded. "Melissa won't be taking group lessons, only private—at least once the trainer starts accepting private students. We expect her to win the championship at the show this summer."

"I see. I imagine something can be arranged."

Mrs. Tolbert tapped her fingers against her crossed arms. "You'll get back to me after you've spoken to your trainer about those lessons?"

"Of course." Mom dipped her head in a brief nod. "If Melissa wants to turn her horse out in the arena to stretch his legs, we'll get the paperwork done. Would you follow me to the office?"

Mom and Mrs. Tolbert headed down the alleyway while Kate and Tori stood frozen in place. Kate motioned toward a nearby stall but didn't meet Melissa's eyes. "We got this stall ready for your horse. You can put him in now, or turn him loose in the arena like my mom suggested. It's up to you." She didn't wait for a response but grabbed Tori's arm and dragged her toward the outer barn door. "Let's get out of here," she hissed.

Kate dashed beside her friend down the aisle that separated the stalls from the indoor arena, then skidded to a stop at the door. She gave it a shove, and they stepped out into the bright sunlight of the clear June day. A horse nickered, and a fly buzzed past her nose, but she ignored them both.

Disaster had struck.

She couldn't imagine how she'd survive the next couple of months with Melissa Tolbert hanging out at their barn.

Tori's eyes brimmed with tears, and she swiped at them with the back of her hand. "She's going to ruin our whole summer. She acts like I don't exist at school … or anywhere."

"I know." Kate trudged over to a stack of straw bales and sank down on one. "But it looks like we're stuck with her."

"Maybe she'll find another place to keep her horse." Tori plunked down on the bale next to Kate.

"Yeah." Kate tore off a piece of straw and stuck it between her teeth. "Except that means we'll lose the money. Mom's pretty excited that we have four boarders, but we need more. Hopefully someone new will come in soon."

"Man, this stinks. Of all the girls at school, we had to land Melissa."

Kate leaned back on her elbows, enjoying the sun warming her face. "Other girls she hangs out with are just as bad."

"I know. At least Melissa's the only one who came. I sure hope none of her friends decide to hang out here with her."

"Yeah. So what do we do now?"

Tori tipped her head to the side. "We can't let her treat us like her slaves."

Kate sighed. "She'll be ordering us around, expecting us to wait on her."

"Will your mom make us do that?"

"I'm not sure, but we're supposed to be grooms and muck stalls. If Mom asks us to do something for her, we might have to."

Tori groaned. "Yuck."

"I know." Even the idea made Kate angry. She tried to shove the anger away. She needed to keep a good attitude. From the beginning she'd known people might come that she wouldn't like, but she'd never envisioned Melissa. Maybe this boarding stable idea wasn't so great after all.

Just then Rufus raced around the corner chasing a stray cat. The big dog dashed inside the barn after the cat, his deep-throated bark echoing off the walls.

Kate and Tori sprang to their feet and ran after him. Kate cupped her hands around her mouth. "Rufus! Come back here, you bad dog."

Tori reached the door a second before Kate. "That's not one of your cats, is it?"

"No. He knows to leave our cats alone. But how'd he get loose? Mom tied him up when the horse trailer got here. She didn't want him scaring a horse."

A girl's scream pierced the air, followed by a thud of hooves hitting a wooden surface.

Kate's heart raced faster than her feet had seconds before. Another high scream sent chills up her spine.

Melissa.

Chapter Four

Kate slowed to a halt a few feet inside the barn door, and Tori bumped into her. Kate grunted. While they'd been outside talking, Melissa must have turned her gelding into the indoor arena.

The cat had leaped over the half wall separating the arena from the alleyway that ran along the front of the stalls, and Rufus had followed it inside. Melissa's big Thoroughbred gelding, Mocha, galloped around the enclosed area, bucking and lashing out with his hooves.

Melissa stood in the center, gripping a lead rope and screaming, "Get out of here, you horrid dog. Leave my horse alone!" She lunged at the dog and swung the rope hard as he raced by. Rufus totally ignored the horse but stayed close to the cat's tail. The rope snaked out and caught him hard on the hindquarters, and Rufus let out a yip.

"Hey, stop hitting my dog!" Kate ran through the open half door into the arena. Mocha raced around the corner at the far end, fury making his legs pump faster.

Kate would have liked nothing better than to get her hands on that rope and ... She checked her runaway thoughts, suddenly ashamed of the direction they'd taken. She wouldn't like her horse to be chased by a strange dog either, but Mom or she should discipline him, not Melissa. Kate shot up a little prayer. *God, please help me control my temper.*

She raised her voice, hoping to be heard above the barking. "Rufus—come here, boy." Melissa's continued shrieks seemed to upset her horse even more. Kate cupped her hands around her mouth. "Leave that cat alone!"

Mom and Mrs. Tolbert ran down the alleyway from the office at the far end of the barn. Mom arrived at their side first. "Rufus, get over here right now," she commanded. "Come."

Something about her voice must have gotten the dog's attention. He slid to a halt only a couple of yards from where Mom stood. He panted and grinned as though he'd won some kind of special doggy award. "I said, come!" She patted her leg, and Rufus trotted over and sat beside her. Grabbing his collar, she led him out into the alleyway. "Kate, tie up your dog. He can't be loose anymore during business hours."

Kate couldn't believe she'd heard right. This was *not* Rufus's fault—or hers. It was that dumb cat's fault for running in front of him, and Melissa's for chasing him and getting her horse all worked up. "Mom! That's mean. I understand keeping him tied up if someone is here, but not all the time!"

"No, young lady, it's not. We can't have him chasing horses."

"But he wasn't. He was chasing a stray cat."

Mrs. Tolbert stepped up and glanced from the dog to her daughter. "Is Mocha all right?"

Melissa stormed across the arena, her mouth pinched in a frown. "You need to discipline that dog and keep him chained. He's dangerous."

Kate pulled Rufus to her side, her hands shaking. "He didn't hurt your horse, and you know it. He wasn't even looking at Mocha. All he cared about was the cat."

"It doesn't matter. Mocha could've hurt himself when he kicked the wall, or he could have hurt someone else." She turned to her mother. "This is what I was afraid of. They don't know what they're doing. I want to take Mocha somewhere else."

"Yeah, well, he could've ruined our wall too." Kate tugged on Rufus's collar and headed toward Tori, who stood quietly a short way up the aisle. "Why don't you find another barn if you think we're so horrible?"

"Kate." Her mother's tone stopped Kate in her tracks. "You need to apologize."

"Mom! I didn't do anything wrong."

"Melissa and her mother are our boarders. They have every right to be upset that Rufus frightened their horse, and you shouldn't be rude."

It was all Kate could do not to glare at her mother, but she knew exactly where that would get her. As it was, she'd probably be grounded for the rest of her life if she didn't follow orders. Even then, she'd bet Mom and Dad would give her a talking to after everyone left. She kicked at a pebble in the dirt, then raised her eyes toward Melissa. "Sorry."

Her mother took a step toward her, eyebrows raised. "Excuse me?"

Tears of humiliation sprang to Kate's eyes. She stared at the wall and blinked a couple of times, then turned toward the arena. "I apologize for saying you should go somewhere else, Melissa."

There. She'd said it the way her mother expected, but she didn't mean it. Not a word. In fact, she hoped Melissa wouldn't accept it. Maybe she would demand they take her horse and leave, and her mother would listen. Nothing would make Kate happier.

Melissa's gelding had come to a stop and stood quietly along the nearby rail. The girl snapped the lead line on the halter and led him to the open gate, stopping only feet from Kate. "Fine. I'm sure you'll make it up to me by grooming my horse when I can't come. But I'll have to show you what I expect and how I want it done."

Kate bit back a moan and curled her fingers into fists. She spun on her heel and glanced at her mother. "I'll take care of Rufus." She stomped down the alleyway past the stalls, with Rufus trailing on his leash behind her. Poor boy. His tail was tucked between his legs. She understood exactly how he felt. They were both doomed to a life of torture for the rest of the summer. Or at least as long as *that girl* chose to keep her horse at their barn.

Minutes later she returned to rescue Tori. Kate realized she never should have left her friend in the barn when she'd taken Rufus to the house. At least Melissa was putting her horse in the stall, and Kate wouldn't have to talk to her again.

Tori stepped out of a stall farther down the alleyway, and Kate heaved a sigh of relief. It looked like her friend had been smart and kept out of Melissa's way, although the other girl was now exiting the stall a few yards away.

Right then Pete shuffled down the long alleyway toward them, his head bent and eyes gazing at his feet. "Hey, Pete." Kate moved forward and held out her hand.

He stopped but didn't move to take it. "Pete wants Rufus."

Kate bent down, not touching her little brother but hoping he'd look up. "Pete, I had to put Rufus in the house. He got loose and scared a horse, and that's not good."

"No. Pete untied Rufus. He wasn't happy."

Kate sagged, shooting a glare at Melissa.

The girl's hard expression had softened to one of under-standing, and she moved forward. "Hi, Pete. I'm Melissa."

Pete didn't move, but his chin lifted ever so slightly. Kate was shocked at Melissa's gentle, tender tone. She'd never heard her speak in anything other than a brittle or demanding voice. "Pete's my brother, and he didn't understand about Rufus and the horses." She said it a little defensively, but she didn't care. One apology to this girl was enough, and no matter how nice Melissa was acting now, Kate bet she'd change her tune when it sank in that Pete had caused the mishap with Mocha. No way would she let Melissa be mean to her brother.

Melissa nodded. "I can see that." She moved closer to Pete, then knelt in front of him. "Do you like dogs, Pete?"

He nodded but didn't look at her.

"I have a puppy I'm training. He goes with me sometimes, so he'll get used to new places. Would you like it if I brought him to see you? He'd have to stay on his leash, but you could pet him and play with him, if you want to."

Pete peeked at her, and a tiny smile twitched. "Uh-huh."

"Good." Melissa rocked back on her heels and grinned. Then she turned her attention to Kate and Tori, and her expres-sion hardened again. "I get it now why your dog got out, but I still don't think this place is run the way it should be. I certainly hope we won't have more problems in the future."

Kate gaped at her, totally knocked sideways at the change in Melissa's behavior. "Yeah. Whatever. Come on, Pete. We'll make sure Rufus is okay." She held out her hand, but the boy walked ahead of her. Of all the rotten things to happen. Sure, she was glad Melissa was nice to Pete. Kate wouldn't want it any other way. But why did her little brother, who didn't respond to anybody, have to respond to a girl who was determined to make life miserable for the rest of them?

Chapter Five

Kate slapped the palms of her hands against her jeans, and a cloud of dust rose. Whew. It looked like she'd been rolling in dirty straw, not merely mucking stalls and putting fresh bedding in them. At least all the horses had been fed and watered, and she could go inside and sit for a while.

Tori was lucky. Her mom had picked her up before the stalls were finished. Kate rinsed her hands under a faucet, loving the feel of cool water running over her newly formed blisters. The barn had been open for over a week, and it felt as if all she did was muck stalls; feed, water, and turn out horses; and run errands. She hadn't even gotten to ride Capri today.

She marched into the house and stopped in the kitchen. Her mother stood at the sink peeling potatoes, and Pete sat in a chair at the dining table, rocking and humming the same tune as always, over and over. Kate ruffled his hair, but he pulled back and didn't look at her. "Hi, Pete. You happy today?"

He kept rocking and humming, staring blankly at a spot on the ceiling.

Kate shrugged. She was glad he wasn't stressed about something and screaming—or banging his head against a wall. "Mom?"

Her mother glanced at her. "Hi, hon. All finished?"

"Yeah."

"Did you make sure the main doors are locked, and the lights are off?"

"Yeah." Kate slouched into a chair across from Pete, trying to block out the humming. "I'm tired. It's not fair that I have to do so much of the work. I didn't get to ride Capri at all today."

Her mother stilled, set the knife on the cutting board next to the sink, then slowly pivoted toward her. "I'm sorry you're tired and you didn't get to ride. But Dad's working late, and I need help setting the table and getting Pete ready for bed."

"Aw, Mom." Kate planted her elbows on the table and huffed.

"Don't cop an attitude with me, Kate. I'm tired too."

"But you spent most of the day with Pete and here in the house."

Mom pulled out a chair and sat. "I could give you a list of the things I've had to deal with today, but I shouldn't have to do that. Maybe we need to talk about shutting down the barn.

It sounds like it's too much for you, and you're already losing interest. Is that the case?"

Kate jerked upright. That was the last thing she wanted. Had her grumbling made Mom think she didn't want to keep the barn open? "No way. I haven't lost interest, and I don't want to quit. I just don't think it's fair that I have to do so much work. Tori and Colt got to go home way early today, and I finished alone."

"Tell me something, Kate. What has Tori gotten out of helping with the chores?"

Kate opened her mouth, all set to give her mother a list, but nothing came out. She snapped her lips shut and twisted them to the side as she struggled to come up with a good answer.

Her mother nodded. "Exactly. Tori is helping because you're her best friend. And Colt does what he agreed to do for his board. There's no reason he should do more."

"Yeah, but Tori knows when we get a lesson horse someday, she'll get to ride it." Kate felt a small degree of triumph. "She'll get free lessons, and we'll even pay for the hay. So that's something."

Mom sighed. "How many people do you know who would clean up around here and do chores several days a week in the hope they'd get to use a lesson horse 'someday'?"

Kate slumped in her seat, all the anger oozing out of her. "You're right. Guess I didn't think about it like that."

"Well, you need to. Tori is kind to help at all. We can't afford to pay her, and she's willing to come so she can hang out with you. That's a pretty generous friend, if you ask me." She pushed to her feet. "And I promise you won't have to do it alone very often. I know that's too much to ask. Thankfully, two of our boarders chose partial care, but when we get more who want full care, we may have to hire a part-time worker. Now change out of those dirty clothes, wash up, and help me get supper on the table."

"All right." Kate stood. "I'm sorry for complaining so much. I really am happy we have the barn, and I'll let Tori know how much I appreciate her."

Her mother gathered Kate into her arms, giving her a long hug. Usually Kate felt too old for mushy stuff, but right now it felt awfully good. Mom wasn't mad at her. Better yet, complaining about doing so much work hadn't made her mother change her mind about the barn. Kate wrapped her arms around her mother and hugged her back, suddenly thankful for all the good things in her life—even for her little brother and the tune he kept humming.

A couple of days later, Kate, Tori, and Colt leaned on the wooden rail fence in the outdoor arena watching Colt's Quarter horse gelding, Romeo, a stunning bay with white socks, canter around the arena kicking up his heels after being released from the horse trailer.

Colt grinned. "Romeo sure is happy to be here, and I am too. Your barn is going to be a lot more fun than the one I was at when Romeo first arrived from Montana."

Kate's interest perked. "What was wrong with that one?"

He shook his head. "The owners at Mountain View Equestrian were great, and the people were friendly. But it was a lot more expensive than yours, and I heard the price went up again. That's the main reason I left. The other reason was the trainer who led the Pony Club and a couple of the members were kind of snooty." He glanced around, then leaned toward them and lowered his voice. "Melissa used to board her horse there."

Tori straightened. "Why isn't she still there?"

Kate grimaced, wishing yet again that Melissa had chosen anywhere else to go but here. "We should tell her your spot is open at the other place you just left. She sure doesn't want to be here."

Colt shrugged. "I'm not sure why she isn't happy here. All I know is the place where she used to be is very particular about everything. All the members of the Pony Club have to do a lot of extra stuff with their horses. They're expected to clean their stalls out two or three times a day—well, not totally clean, but strip them once and pick them the other two times when they need it. They scrubbed their water buckets every day, brushed their horses' manes and kept ShowSheen on them so they didn't tangle, kept polish on their horses' hooves, and lots more stuff. I wasn't part of their group, so they didn't make me do it all. A lot of the kids looked down on me because I wasn't taking care of my horse the exact same way they were.

"I cleaned my horse's stall once a day, but he was turned out for several hours in an outside paddock when I couldn't ride, so it wasn't like he was standing around all the time. And his mane is supershort—I keep it pulled—so he didn't need ShowSheen."

Kate's eyes widened. "Wow! That's crazy! I don't see why they require all of that. I mean, it's your horse, and you should do what you think is best. As long as you're feeding and watering and exercising him, of course. No horse should be neglected, but it sounds like they expected a lot."

Colt nodded. "That's what I thought. The barn's owners didn't have rules, but they supported the club. I don't imagine it helped that I homeschool, and I'm not one of their crowd either. Not that they were ever mean. I was mostly ignored and treated like I didn't know much or didn't exist."

Tori rolled her eyes at Kate. "Sounds like how Melissa treats us at school. You suppose it has anything to do with her being part of that crowd?"

Kate gave a slow nod. "I suppose it could. But I still don't get why she's not there if she liked it so much. I thought she'd leave for sure after she got upset about Rufus spooking her horse in the arena the day she came." She glanced at Colt. "Did Tori tell you about that?"

"Nope. What's the deal with Rufus?" He dug in his pocket and extracted something, then held it out to his horse. The gelding snuffled, his nostrils flaring, and snatched the treat from Colt's open palm. "Greedy, aren't you?" Colt chuckled and pulled out another treat.

"What's that?" Tori asked.

"Homemade horse treats. Mom and I make them, and Romeo loves them."

Kate peered at the brown treat lying on Colt's palm. "Cool. Give us the recipe."

He offered the last one to Romeo, then swung around and glanced from Kate to Tori. "What did I miss with Melissa?"

Kate sighed, hating to admit Rufus had been in the wrong, but she had to be fair. "My dog got loose. In fact, we found out Pete untied him, but Pete didn't understand. We're supposed to keep Rufus in the house or tied up while horses are out or boarders are riding in the arena, at least until he learns what's off limits. But he got into the arena while Melissa's horse was there, and she totally came unglued! I mean, she lost it big time.

She was running around screaming at Rufus, hitting him with her lead rope, and acting all crazy." She shook her head. "Rufus was wrong, but I think she overreacted. And Mom made *me* apologize."

Colt wrinkled his brows. "Why? What did you do wrong?"

Kate's shoulders slumped as the memory returned. "I guess I got a little mouthy. At least Mom thought I did. Okay, I kind of did. Melissa made me mad."

Tori hitched a little closer to Kate. "I didn't blame Kate for the way she reacted. I mean, Melissa isn't the easiest girl to be around, and she's not a bit friendly. She'd already made it super-clear she didn't think this barn was good enough for her horse, and she didn't want to be here."

Colt turned around, his back to the fence and his elbows propped on either side. "There's something I should probably tell you about Melissa."

Chapter Six

Kate narrowed her eyes, wondering at Colt's tone. "Tell us about Melissa. How well do you know her?"

Colt leaned over, plucked a blade of coarse grass, and stuck it between his teeth. "Not well, but I can probably explain why she freaked out when your dog spooked her horse."

Tori's brows rose. "I know she was worried Rufus might hurt Mocha, even though that didn't seem likely. Was there another reason?"

He shifted the grass to the other side of his mouth. "Yeah. She got unloaded a few weeks ago."

Tori wrinkled her nose. "Unloaded? I don't get it."

"Dumped. Bucked off her horse."

Kate cocked her head. "But what does that have to do with Rufus?" None of this made sense, but she was willing to listen.

"She was riding in the outdoor arena. Apparently her last gelding got spooked easily. One of the barn cats took off at a dead run through the arena and darted right under Melissa's horse. He didn't run over the cat, but it scared him half to death, and he started bucking. She's a good rider, but it was so sudden, she must not have had time to prepare. She got launched and landed pretty hard. I kinda wonder if that's why they sold him. She went without a horse the rest of the time I was there. Maybe that's why she's here—they may have rented her stall to someone else."

Kate winced. "Ouch. Was she hurt bad?"

"She got the wind knocked out of her, the same as Tori when she fell off Capri. But she probably hit a lot harder. It's a good thing the arena had been plowed the day before and was soft. Plus, she was wearing her helmet, or she could have had a serious head injury."

Tori nodded. "That's what my mom told me. Her brother got hurt the same way years ago, and he wasn't wearing a helmet. She told me she'll never allow me to ride unless I have one on at all times."

"Yeah," Colt said. "That's one of the rules at Mountain View Equestrian Center. You wear a helmet, or you don't ride."

Kate smiled. "We decided that before we opened our barn. Mom said the insurance would be sky-high if we didn't. New boarders have to sign an agreement. But how about Melissa? What happened?"

"People caught her horse and checked her out. She got her breath back and stood, but she was pretty wobbly. She wanted to get back in the saddle, but the owner wouldn't let her. Said she needed to have her mother take her to the doctor."

"Did she?" Tori asked.

"I don't know. She left right after that and didn't come to the barn again for a few days. I think it spooked her so bad, she was afraid to get back on. I've heard of that happening."

Kate felt sick. "Now I see why she got so mad. She wasn't on Mocha, but it must have brought back bad memories. Now I feel awful for getting angry at her. I've heard you're supposed to get back on a horse as soon as you get dumped, or you might lose your nerve and not ride again. Do you know if Melissa still rides?"

"Don't know for sure. Not long after, I switched to the other barn where you guys worked. We couldn't afford Mountain View, and I had a chance to work off part of my board instead of taking lessons, like you. It was a nice barn and I would have stayed there, but it's going to be more hanging out with friends here."

Kate shuddered. Would Tori have the same problem now that she'd fallen off a large horse and refuse to ride again? "We'll have to be nicer to Melissa when she comes." She turned to Tori. "Want to see if Mom will help you ride Capri? She can make her go slow, and I'll walk along beside her if you want.

I'll bet Colt would even ride at the same time in the arena. It would be fun!"

Tori gazed with wide eyes from Kate to Colt and back. "Thanks, but not today. Maybe next time I come, okay?"

Kate's heart took a dive toward her riding boots and seemed to stay there. Her best friend was afraid of horses, and it was all her fault. And now Melissa was afraid as well, and she wasn't even a friend. Trouble sure came all at once lately. Kate hoped this was all the trouble they would have to deal with for now. She couldn't take a lot more.

A few days later, Kate bounced up and down, giddy with excitement. Grabbing Tori's hand, she swung her around in a circle. "Can you believe we get our first lessons with our new trainer today? I can't wait!"

Tori loosened her fingers from Kate's and smiled. "I'm going to watch this time. It's not like you have a lesson horse yet. As soon as you do, I'll take lessons here, since we aren't taking them at the other barn anymore."

Kate stopped in her tracks. "Tori, I'm so sorry. Why didn't I think of that?" She slapped her forehead. "I've got to talk to

Mom about finding a lesson horse. I know we'd use one a lot, and it would earn its keep if we did. It's not fair that you're working here and not getting anything out of it." A sudden idea swept away the guilt, and she clapped her hands. "I know! I'll do the first half of the hour on Capri. By then she'll be tired and behaving herself, and you can use her the second half, okay?"

Tori shook her head. "Nuh-uh. No way am I robbing you of your first full lesson with our new trainer. You've looked forward to this for weeks. I can wait till next time."

Kate studied her friend. Tori was one of the kindest, most generous people she knew, but was this refusal coming from that or because she was still afraid to ride? Just a couple of days ago, they'd gone back to their old barn, since the owner still owed them an hour lesson for the work they'd done before giving notice. Tori had climbed on Lulu reluctantly but didn't refuse. Of course, Lulu was a lot smaller than Capri, but that didn't mean Tori would want to get back on Capri anytime soon.

Kate narrowed her eyes at Tori. "Do you promise to ride Capri half the lesson next time and keep doing it until we get a good lesson horse?"

Tori hesitated, then nodded. "I promise." She grinned. "As long as nothing bad happens between now and then."

Kate shivered even though she knew Tori was joking. "Nothing's going to happen. I even saw Melissa riding Mocha in the indoor arena." She frowned. "Only at a walk and trot for about thirty minutes, but at least she's riding him. That's positive."

Tori smiled. "I'm glad. She hasn't been mean lately either. In fact, she said hi to me recently."

"Wow! That's a huge improvement!" Kate beamed at Tori and linked arms with her. "Come on, let's go tack up Capri. Colt should be here for the Western lesson by the time the English one is half over." She winked at Tori. "I can't believe how insulted he was when we told him he should ride English."

"I know." Tori giggled. "'Are you kidding? Me in a pair of breaches? I'd quit riding before I'd wear a pair of those things.'" She did a nearly perfect imitation of Colt's voice.

Kate broke out in a full laugh as she tugged Tori toward the tack room. "I'd have my camera handy if he did! Come on, we don't have a lot of time to get ready."

An hour and a half later, Kate, Tori, and Colt stood at the low rail separating the alleyway from the indoor arena, enthralled at the sight playing out before them. Kate sucked in a quick breath. "My lesson was great, but I want to learn to jump! Capri is trained for it, but I'm not. I'm going to ask Mom when I can start taking lessons that teach more than flat work. It's not like I don't have the basics down."

Colt gave a lopsided grin. "Yeah, but there's a lot more to jumping than leaning forward and letting your horse pop over the rails. I don't ride English, but I've watched it at the other two barns where I boarded my horse. From what I've seen, you've got to have supersteady hands, excellent balance, the ability to post and change leads easily, and a sense of timing for the jumps."

Tori gazed at him openmouthed. "Wow. You know a lot."

A slow flush climbed from his neck to his cheeks, and Colt ducked his head. "Nah. It's hard not to hear stuff when you're cleaning stalls right next to the arena. I always seemed to be there when jumping lessons took place, that's all."

Kate turned to the arena again. "It's not a very big class yet. Just four riders. Melissa and three women I don't know. One of them boards her mare here, and I think Mom said the other two trailered their horses in for the lesson. Melissa's mom agreed to let her take a group lesson to start, then she's going to take private ones after this." She grinned at her friends. "That should be way cool!"

Tori huffed. "Those jumps aren't very high. The horses can practically step over them. What are they, about two feet, if that?"

Kate nodded. "Eighteen inches. The instructor can raise the height of the rails all the way up to six feet if she wants to, but she told Mom she plans to start everyone out low, even if they say they know what they're doing and want to go higher."

Colt leaned a hip against the low wall. "Smart lady. Make sure, so she doesn't have accidents. What's her name anyway? Is she well known in the valley?"

"Mrs. Jamison," Kate said. "She moved here from Portland recently. I guess she got tired of city life and wanted to be in a more rural area but still somewhere there's a lot of interest in dressage and jumping. Mom checked her out, and she has a good reputation. We put ads in the local paper to let the public know about the classes. I wish we'd gotten a better response for this first lesson, but Mrs. Jamison didn't seem to mind."

Colt gave a soft grunt. "If she's good, word will get out, and more people will come. It won't take long."

Tori leaned in closer, staring at the arena as Melissa's gelding increased his pace to a slow gallop and cleared a jump. "At least Melissa's riding again—and jumping. She must not have been as scared as we thought." She frowned.

"I can't quite figure her out," Kate said. "Sometimes it's like she wants to be friendly, then quick as a cat, she switches to her old personality." She giggled. "Sorry. It wasn't very nice to compare her to a cat after her accident."

Colt flicked a hand toward the arena. "Looks like Mrs. Jamison is satisfied. She's raising the poles to two and a half feet."

Tori squinted the way he was pointing. "How can you tell?"

"Every jump cup is set three inches apart, so you count the cups and multiply." He grinned and bumped Tori's shoulder. "You do know how to multiply, right?"

Tori swatted his arm. "Watch it, or we'll make you clean *all* the stalls."

He tipped back his head and hooted, then sobered as Mrs. Jamison scowled at him. "Sorry, ma'am." He dropped his voice to a whisper. "I know better than that. I'm glad no one was jumping."

They watched in silence as the instructor finished adjusting the height of the rails, then moved to her place in the center. "All right, everyone. I want Melissa to go first, then Miss Ryan, then Mrs. Hooper, followed by Mrs. Carson. Please trot your horses a half circle around the arena, then increase to a controlled canter and come down the center, taking the three jumps. When you finish, move off to the side and out of the way of the next rider."

Kate watched with interest, wondering if the higher rails would shake Melissa's confidence, or if the girl would take them with ease. Melissa put Mocha into a trot, posting on the inside lead, then transitioned smoothly into a collected canter, her gelding's nose tucked and his neck nicely rounded. Her hands were steady, and she sat the canter as though molded to the horse, moving with the rhythm and looking straight ahead. She rounded the final corner and directed Mocha in a straight line toward the first jump, then tugged on the reins and slowed him as he started to rush.

Kate could hear Melissa's whispered assurance to her mount, then a "hup" a stride before the jump. The dark bay gelding sailed over the rail without even flicking his ears. He got to the second rail and repeated his performance, and Kate began to breathe easy. One rail to go.

The big gelding took two more strides. Melissa was in three-point position, almost standing in her stirrups, her hands gripping the reins forward on Mocha's neck, when all of a sudden he swerved away from the rail, darting out of the jump line.

The quick sideways movement threw Melissa off balance, and she gasped. One foot came out of the stirrup, and she leaned precariously to one side.

Chapter Seven

Mrs. Jamison walked toward the horse, talking in a hushed tone as he continued to canter toward the far side of the arena. She raised her voice a bit. "Melissa, grab his mane and pull yourself upright. That's a good girl. You're doing fine."

Melissa heaved herself the opposite direction and fumbled for her stirrup, then drew back on the reins and brought Mocha to a halt.

Kate knew what was coming next—the explosion of temper she'd seen in the barn when Rufus had frightened Melissa's horse. She'd hate to be an animal that made this girl mad. Kate would bet that any minute the crop Melissa held would flay Mocha's backside.

She didn't realize she'd been holding her breath for several seconds, until she felt the need for air and released it, then sucked air into her lungs. She stared at Melissa, shocked at what she saw. The other girl spoke in a soft, soothing tone, stroking

Mocha's neck and patting him like he'd done something right instead of wrong.

Kate shook her head, not understanding. Where was the Melissa who'd screamed at Rufus the day she arrived? She turned to Colt and Tori, ready to ask what they thought, when Melissa bumped Mocha with her heel and drove him forward into a trot.

Mrs. Jamison didn't speak but moved to the center of the ring and nodded in approval.

Melissa increased her horse's gait to a canter, then rounded the corner and headed for the first jump again. Mocha cleared it and headed toward the second at a steady pace, but what about the third?

Tori leaned closer. "Think he'll go over this time? If I were Melissa, I wouldn't try again. I'd have gotten off that horse."

The awe and respect coloring Tori's voice seared Kate with discomfort. Had Melissa won Tori over like she had Pete? Kate returned her attention to the arena, not wanting to miss the action. Feeling bad over her pang of jealousy, she asked God to keep Mocha steady this time, even though part of her wished Melissa wouldn't have something to brag about later.

Melissa tightened the reins as she neared the third jump, planted her heels even lower, and pressed her fists on each side of Mocha's neck as she gripped the reins. She kissed to the horse a stride before the fence. He slowed for an instant, then rose and soared over as though it wasn't even there.

A muted shout broke from Colt's lips, and even Tori applauded. Kate wasn't sure what to think. If Melissa had been friendlier or even polite most of the time, she'd want to root for the girl too. She was happy Melissa hadn't been thrown and had gotten her confidence back, but part of her squirmed at the accomplishment of this girl who quickly seemed to be turning into a rival—in more ways than one.

Kate worked to maintain a smile, but her heart hurt. Would she lose her two best friends to Melissa, or was she silly to even think that way? After leaving all her friends in Spokane a few months ago, she hated the thought of starting over again. She gave herself a small shake and told herself to knock it off. Just because Pete responded to Melissa, and Colt and Tori thought she'd done a good job, didn't mean any of them intended to desert her.

"She did great, huh?" Kate mustered a smile. "I think I'd better get to work. It's easier to clean the stalls with the horses out, so I'll tackle Mocha's first and then the one for Miss Ryan's mare. You guys can stay here and watch."

She started to move away, but Tori caught her arm. "Hey, wait up. I'd rather spend time with you than watch another lesson. I think my brain is worn out from all the technical stuff

Mrs. Jamison throws at them, anyway." She looped her hand through Kate's arm.

Kate felt like she would burst with joy. She gazed at Tori, then looked at Colt. "How about you?"

"I'm only here because you guys wanted to watch. I took care of my stall already, and I'd better get home. Dad said he needs help building a chicken coop tonight." He exhaled heavily. "I told him I don't mind building it, but I'm not crazy about cleaning it once it's done."

Kate grinned. "Oh, but think about all those yummy eggs and that fried chicken."

Tori shuddered. "That's awful! Poor little baby chicks. They'll grow up and end up on someone's barbecue."

Colt laughed. "Where do you think the chickens come from that are in the store?"

She frowned. "That's different. You don't hold those cute fluff balls and give them names."

Colt rolled his eyes. "And I'm not going to give them names either, you goof." He lifted his hand in a brief wave, then gave an impish smile. "Later, guys. Have fun cleaning stalls without me!"

He ducked out of the way before Kate's slap could connect with his arm, then jogged down the alleyway toward the outer door, laughing the entire way.

"Boys." Tori pulled Kate toward the stall that housed Melissa's horse. Once they had snagged the wheelbarrow, pitchfork, and rake, they entered the stall, and she swung to face Kate. "What gives?"

"Huh?" Kate blinked. "What are you talking about?"

"You got all quiet after Melissa cleared that jump." She studied Kate. "But not until after I clapped, and Colt said she did a good job. Are you jealous of Melissa?"

Kate squirmed, finding it hard to meet Tori's probing gaze. She grabbed a pitchfork and dug into a pile of manure mixed with sawdust, then tossed it into the wheelbarrow. "We'd better get busy. Melissa could be here any minute."

"No way." Tori snatched the fork from Kate's hands. "Not until you tell me what gives. I've never seen you like this before. You don't get mad at the kids at school even if they make a snide remark. I've seen you be kind to her more than once since she's arrived, and now you're acting all weird. Is it because I was happy she didn't fall off her horse again?" She crossed her arms and tapped her foot.

Kate hung her head, feeling horrible that Tori had figured it out. No way could she lie. Besides, what would God think if she did? She already felt bad enough that she'd allowed jealousy to put her in a bad mood, without adding anything else to the pile. "Yeah, I guess so."

Tori relaxed, and her arms swung to her sides. "So you thought I'd ditch you for Melissa? Seriously? I mean, why would I do that? You're my friend. Just because I was happy she didn't get hurt doesn't mean I want her as my new best friend." She snorted a laugh. "I can't even imagine what that would be like. We're about as far apart as two people can be."

"Now isn't that the truth?" a voice drawled from the alleyway a split second before the door rolled open and Melissa paused at the entrance, Mocha behind her on a lead. Kate wanted to crawl off into a pile of straw and bury herself. She could imagine what Tori must be feeling right now. What rotten timing. Tori had been joking. She'd seen it on her friend's face, but Melissa wouldn't know that. More than anything, Tori had hoped to assure Kate of her friendship and loyalty. She'd accomplished that, but Kate was mortified that Melissa had overheard.

Melissa's eyes blazed, and she stood as stiff as the pitchfork handle. "I can't imagine being friends with either of you, or why you'd think I'd care to be. As for being happy I didn't fall off my horse, that's ridiculous. I'm a better rider than the two of you put together, or that silly boyfriend of yours."

Kate's tongue finally loosened. "Colt is not a boyfriend. He's a nice guy who was happy you weren't hurt, like we were."

"It's pretty obvious how happy you both are." Melissa's lip curled. "If I did get hurt before, then I wouldn't be here showing you up with my horse and my riding." She flicked a hand at the stall floor. "I see you don't have this stripped or fresh bedding down yet. At our other barn, our stalls were always ready when we finished riding. And we had rubber mats on the floor, not dirt covered with shavings."

She looked over her shoulder and then up at the rafters. "Everything here is dirty. No rubber mats on the alleyways either. The tack room barely has enough shelves, hooks, or saddle racks for the boarders you have now, and the arena fences need to be repainted. It's all so … rundown and grubby. I don't understand why you couldn't get it fixed up before you opened for business."

Kate didn't trust herself to respond. She bent over and picked up the pitchfork, and Tori grabbed the handles of the wheelbarrow. Kate flicked a glance at Melissa. "We're sorry, Melissa. We'll get done as fast as we can."

Tori choked out a strangled sound. She looked as if she might burst into tears any minute. "I'm sorry too. I didn't mean anything bad. I was trying to make Kate feel better, that's all."

Melissa stepped into the alleyway. "Whatever. I don't care what you meant. I'll cross-tie Mocha out here while you finish. Maybe I'll go talk to your little brother. Pete, right? I saw him outside when I walked past the door." She pivoted and walked away without another word.

Chapter Eight

Kate and Tori didn't discuss what happened after Melissa left, but it was all Kate could think about for the next few days. She made a point of avoiding Melissa when she could and being nice to her when she couldn't, but nothing helped. Was Melissa a snob who only cared about herself, or a girl with something going on inside that made her lash out at people around her? Kate couldn't figure it out. She wasn't sure she even wanted to, but it bugged her all the same.

She sat on her bed Sunday afternoon, happy she'd gotten to ride Capri after church, but something was missing. Maybe she should start praying for Melissa. But how? And what about? That God would make her nicer? That He'd fix whatever was wrong? She shook her head, her braid swinging. She didn't have a clue.

Someone rapped at her door, and she looked up. "Who is it?"

"Your mother. May I come in?"

"Sure." Kate waited till her mom entered the room. "What's up? Do you need help with supper?"

She perched on the edge of the bed by Kate. "That's very kind of you, and yes, I will in a while. But your dad and I noticed you've been awfully quiet lately. Anything you want to talk about?"

"Naw. Thanks for asking, though. Is that all you wanted?" She clenched her hands into fists, wishing she could pour everything out to her mom the way she had when she was little. But she was thirteen now, not a baby. She needed to figure this out on her own.

"There's one other thing, and I hope it will make you feel better." Her mom's hazel eyes smiled into Kate's. "Mrs. Jamison talked to Dad and me. Apparently the hunter-jumper show that was supposed to be held in a big field on the edge of town needs to find a new location. It's not a big show, but it's on the circuit for earning points toward regionals. They hate to cancel it, and the only other barn with an indoor and outdoor arena large enough is booked."

"So …?" Kate held her breath, hoping she'd figured out what might be coming. "Did she ask if we could hold it here?" She rose onto her knees and bounced on the bed, barely able to contain her excitement. "That would be so cool! We'll do it, right? Please, Mom!"

Her mother held up her hand, but a smile tugged at her lips. "Slow down, Kate. It would mean a lot of work. It would help to get our name out to people who don't know we're open, and part of the entry fees would go to us for hosting it, but it's a huge undertaking. And we only have three weeks."

"Three weeks? Yikes!" Kate sank against her pillow. "What all would we have to do?"

"The committee handles all the advertising, but we'd need to have the stalls we're not using cleaned out and bedded. The pastures would have to be cross-fenced with temporary hot-wire tape so horses could be turned out, since there's no way we'll have enough stalls. A lot of the owners will keep their horses tied to their trailers, but not everyone wants to do that. Plus, general cleanup and sprucing up areas we haven't gotten to yet."

Kate gave a slow nod, remembering Melissa's retort. "Maybe we tried to open too soon. I guess there's still a lot to do, even though I thought we were ready."

"Yes, and I'm glad you can see that. We were all caught in the excitement of taking in boarders and getting a trainer, and we probably shouldn't have rushed, but that's in the past. Right now we have to decide if we can tackle this new project." Her eyes shone, but Kate could see her mother wavering.

"I say yes, and I'll bet Tori and Colt will both help too. Maybe we'd even make enough to buy a lesson horse that Tori could use. What does Dad think?"

Her mother smiled. "He says it's up to us girls. He'll do all he can to help us get ready, and he'll watch Pete during the show. We have a little extra money right now, so we can buy nicer jumps for the competition. The committee provides all the ribbons and the top prize, a set of English silver spurs to the person with the highest points overall."

"Silver spurs?" Kate breathed the words. "Awesome. I'm all for it. How about you, Mom?" She waited, hardly daring to hope. Her first show. She wasn't ready to jump, but she could compete in the flat classes like hunt-seat, equitation, or English pleasure, and she might even have a chance at a ribbon or two.

Mom grinned and drew Kate into a hug. "I say if you're up for it, so am I. You've been a trooper doing so much work around here. We're going to make this barn a success! Just pray we don't have any accidents and that nothing goes wrong. Having a rated show at our barn is an awesome opportunity, and we don't want to blow it."

Two nights later, Kate was in her pajamas trying to read over the screaming wind. She'd just hung up the phone after telling

Tori they'd bought new jumps, and the show would for sure be at their barn.

The weather forecast had called for high winds, but she hadn't expected anything like this. At least living in Odell they'd missed some of the stronger winds that tore through the Columbia River Gorge that acted like a funnel, either directing winds to the east toward the desert or west toward Portland. Either way, they could be brutal.

The windsurfers loved the wind, but Kate was already tired of it. She'd heard that midsummer was better, and spring through early summer was the worst. She hoped that was the case.

All of a sudden, something crashed outside, not terribly far from the house. It almost sounded like an explosion. Kate jumped from her bed and raced to her door. She yanked it open and hollered down the stairs. "Mom? Dad? What was that? Is everything okay?"

She heard the front door slam, and boots thudded down the front porch stairs. Kate clumped downstairs, praying the barn and horses were fine. "Mom? Did Dad go outside? Is Pete still asleep, or did it wake him up?"

Her mother met her in the living room, worry clouding her face. "I'm not sure what's going on. Pete can sleep through almost anything, but I'll go check anyway. Your dad took the big flashlight and went outside to look around."

Kate headed for the front door. No way was she getting left behind if something exciting had happened—especially not if Capri or any of the other horses were in danger. She reached for the front door with one hand and her coat hanging on a peg with the other.

"Hold it, young lady." Her mother grabbed Kate's shoulder and swung her around. "You're not to go outside. Dad's orders. Wait for him to come in." Kate opened her mouth to protest, but her mom insisted. "No argument. Promise me now, or I'll make *you* go check on Pete, and I'll stay here." She had that determined glint in her eyes that Kate knew so well.

"All right. Fine. I promise. But I don't like it. What if Capri is hurt?" She ran to a front window and looked out toward the barn, but no moon shone, and it was pitch-dark. She could see a flashlight beam bobbing not far away, but she didn't see what had caused the teeth-jarring noise.

"Your dad will tell us as soon as he gets in. Until then, stay put." She shook her finger at Kate. "I'll be right back. I don't see how Pete could sleep through all this racket."

Kate continued to peek out the window, dying to know what was happening. Would Mom freak if she opened the front door and hollered at Dad? Probably. She'd better not push her luck, especially since she didn't know if it was safe to step outside. But what if Capri was seriously hurt? She didn't care about the show or anything else right now. As long as Capri was okay, she'd give up entering every competition for the rest of her life.

She closed her eyes. "Please, God. Please, please, please. Let Capri and all the other horses be safe." Footsteps echoed on the front porch, and her eyes flew open in the hope that God had answered her prayer.

When she jerked open the door, Dad almost tumbled inside, with his arm extended and a surprised look on his face. "Dad! How's Capri? Is she safe? How about the rest of the horses? What was that awful sound? Did something explode?"

Mom rushed into the room without Pete and stopped beside Kate. She wrapped her arm around Kate's shoulders. "Slow down, honey. Give your dad a chance to catch his breath."

Dad shrugged out of his coat. "Capri is fine, and so are the rest of the horses. No damage to the barn, thankfully."

Kate expelled a hard breath. "Thank You, God." Her mother raised her brows. "I mean it, Mom. I prayed while you were upstairs. I'm so glad the horses aren't hurt." She refocused on her father. "So what exploded?"

"Our big fir tree that's been dying. I should have taken it down, but I kept putting it off. The wind was so strong, it broke off the top half of the tree, and it landed on the outdoor arena."

"Oh no!" Mom covered her mouth with her hand. "How bad is it?"

He met her gaze with a steady one of his own. "Not good, but I can't tell for sure in the dark. It took out some of the fence, and it's on top of a number of the jumps."

"The old ones or the new ones we bought today?"

"I won't know till tomorrow."

Kate groaned. "What are we going to do? The show is in three weeks. All the jumping classes are supposed to take place in the outdoor arena, since the flat classes are indoors. And we have to have the jumps, or we won't have a show!" She grabbed her coat, then reached for the flashlight.

Her dad put his hand over hers. "Not tonight, Kate. There's nothing we can do. Without good light, we can't see anything. And it would be too easy to get hurt if we tried. I don't know if the tree is stable, or if it's hanging up on something and could roll or fall. We don't go near it until morning. Understood?"

Kate nodded, but it took all her willpower not to snatch the light and race out to check for herself. They couldn't cancel the show, they just couldn't! This might be their only opportunity to get included in a rated show. She was pretty sure they didn't have the money to replace the fence or the jumps. Why did this have to happen now, when the show was so close?

Chapter Nine

Kate lay in bed early the next morning, her body tired and her brain muddled. She hadn't slept soundly but couldn't quite remember why. Then she sat upright with a start. *The windstorm. The tree. The damaged fence and jumps!*

Kate bolted out of bed, threw on her jeans, shirt, and socks, then headed downstairs. "Mom? Dad?" She hurried from one room to the other. Pete would still be in bed, and her parents must be outside inspecting the damage.

Tugging on her boots, Kate let her mind scurry ahead. Could the fence be repaired without too much cost? And what about the jumps? She dreaded even thinking about those. When she whipped open the door, she was thankful the wind had calmed.

Rufus bounded around a corner and leaped onto the porch. He nudged Kate's hand before heading back the way he'd come. "Wait up, boy."

Kate broke into a jog and didn't slow her pace until the huge fir tree came into view. The bottom half still stood, but it ended in a jagged, splintered mess, no longer a towering, majestic tree.

Mom and Dad stood by the downed top half, and Mom's face looked as if she'd been crying. Kate stopped beside her parents and surveyed the scene. Broken branches littered a large area of the grass, pasture, and the inside of the arena. But that was the least of the problem. The base of the part that had snapped had landed on the end of the arena fence, completely obscuring any sign of it.

She looped her arm through her mother's. "How come Dad isn't at work? How bad is it? The jumps, I mean. I can tell the fence is trashed."

Her mother squeezed Kate's hand against her side. "Not good. Dad called his boss and doesn't have to come in until noon. He'll get his chain saw and cut branches off before we know for sure. At this point we've been able to spot one jump that's shattered. This entire end of the arena will have to be rebuilt, and some large branches broke a few boards on the far side as well."

Kate tried to swallow the lump in her throat. "How about the show?"

Dad stuffed his hands in the pockets of his jeans. "I was telling your mom that we may have to contact the head of the show committee and cancel."

"But, Dad, the committee already put ads in the paper, and notices have been emailed! It's not fair to cancel. There's got to be some way we can still hold it."

He shook his head. "I think most of the jumps are damaged or destroyed, along with a big section of fence. We don't have the money to repair and replace everything that soon. I wish we did, but we don't. I'm beginning to wonder if we made the wrong decision to open in the first place."

Kate gulped down a harsh protest, knowing it wouldn't help to be critical. Her mother had already been crying, and it wasn't fair to either of her parents to blame them if they didn't have the money. But it hurt regardless.

She kicked at a fir cone, then looked up. "Can we wait till you get the branches cut and see for sure? It might not be as bad as you think."

Her dad hesitated. "I suppose so. It's too early to call anyone now anyway. I'll grab the chain saw. Nan, want to throw some breakfast together? Kate, how about you check on Pete and help your mother in the kitchen?"

"Can't I stay here and help you? I have leather gloves, and I'm strong enough to move branches."

"I know you are, kiddo. There will be plenty of branches to move after breakfast. I won't be able to tell anything for a while. I have to sharpen the chain and get the saw running first. I haven't used it since we moved here."

"Okay." Kate stroked Rufus's head as he pressed close, seeming to sense her emotions. "Come on, boy. Let's get you fed and help Mom."

Twenty minutes later the saw roared to life, and Kate ran to the window. Dad stood shaking his head in the middle of the arena where the top of the tree lay. Kate's heart sank. It must be worse than they'd thought.

After breakfast Kate, Pete, and her parents walked outside and headed for the tree, equipped with rakes, gloves, and the chain saw. Kate wished she could grab that stupid tree and yank it off the fence with her bare hands, but that was silly. From the look of the mess, this could take all day to clean up—or longer. She hadn't stopped praying all through breakfast that somehow the jumps would be fine.

A car turned off the road into their driveway, and Kate let out a whoop. "Tori's here!"

Her mother smiled. "Since Tori isn't old enough to drive, I assume one of her parents is with her. I hope it's her mother. I haven't seen her in a while."

The car rolled to a stop, and three people emerged—Tori, her father, and her mother. Tori's father carried a chain saw, and all of them had leather gloves.

Kate gaped at the family, then ran forward and hugged Tori. She pulled away a couple of inches but retained her hold on her friend. "What are you guys doing? How did you know we needed help?"

Tori slipped out of Kate's hold. "One of Mom and Dad's friends lives on the property that is next to yours." She waved at a white two-story, the Ferrises' nearest neighbor, only about a hundred feet from the far end of the arena. "They heard a loud crash last night and got up early to see what it was. When they heard your dad's saw this morning, they drove by and saw the tree. They know we're friends, so Mrs. Jiménez called Mom and told her what happened. Mr. and Mrs. Jiménez said to tell you they'll be over to help soon."

Dad reached out to Mr. Velasquez and shook hands. "I would never have called you and imposed, but I'm grateful you came. Thank you."

Mom's eyes brimmed with tears, and she sniffed. "I don't know what to say."

Tori's mother gave Kate's mom a quick hug. "You'd do the same if we needed help."

Dad grinned. "Nan, how about you put on a big pot of coffee and bring out a plate of those cinnamon rolls you baked yesterday? Then you ladies can sit and visit or move a few branches, whatever you prefer."

Tori's mom laughed. "I didn't come to eat and visit. I came to work."

Kate's dad pointed to two bare spots in the field not far away. "José and I will cut anything into firewood that's big enough, and the rest of you can take what's left to the proper pile."

A middle-aged Hispanic man and woman ducked through the fence and headed across the short section of pasture bordering the arena. He nodded to Tori's father and extended his hand to Kate's dad. "Samuel Jiménez, and this is my wife, Mary."

"Pleased to meet you, and I'm sorry we haven't met before. I'm John Ferris, and this is my wife, Nan, and my daughter, Kate. Our son, Pete, is inside watching a video."

Kate's father started his saw, and Tori's dad did the same, making any further conversation impossible.

Tori grabbed Kate's hand and drew her off to the side. "What does your dad think about the fence? I saw part of a broken jump under the branches. Do you know if that's the only one?" A frown puckered her forehead.

Kate shook her head, feeling sick all over again. "A bunch of the jumps were near that fence. We put them out there a few days ago so we'd have them ready when they're needed. Now I wish we'd left them in the barn."

"It was a huge windstorm, but it's not like you thought the tree would crash down on top of everything. So what happens if the jumps are all busted?"

Kate winced, not liking the picture that question created in her mind. "Dad says we'll have to call the show coordinator and cancel."

Tori gasped. "Why? Can't you buy new jumps or fix them? We can help repair the fence. My dad's handy with a hammer and nails."

"That's nice of you, but it takes money. More than we have right now. Dad even wondered if we should have opened the barn for business." She dropped her voice to a loud whisper so Tori could still hear. "And Mom looked like she'd been crying when I came out this morning. I thought I was the only one in the family who was looking forward to this show, but I think Mom wanted it to be a success too."

"Man, I'm so sorry."

Kate gave Tori a weak smile. "Thanks. I'm going to tell my folks they can use the two hundred dollars I have in savings from my birthday and from Christmas money my aunts and uncles have sent me the last several years, plus what I've saved from doing extra chores."

"Would that be enough?"

Kate hesitated, wondering if her parents had thought that far. "I know they have close to enough put aside to buy a lesson horse soon, if we can find one at a reasonable price. I wasn't going to tell you because I wanted it to be a surprise. Now I wonder if they should use that money to fix things instead. But we need a good lesson horse if we're going to bring in more people."

Tori nodded. "That's tough. Tell you what—I'll be praying that God sends an answer."

Kate smiled, glad for the gazillionth time that Tori was her best friend. "Thanks. Ready to go drag some branches out of the way?"

Tori grinned. "Lead me to them!"

Two hours later, the majority of the tree had been cut, a nice stack of firewood leaned against the house, and a pile of branches sat in a clear spot where it would be safe to burn. The chain saws were silent, and the crew stood near the broken fence surveying the damage.

Kate gulped back a sob, determined not to cry, but she knew the show was doomed. Most of the old jumps were splintered, and at least three of the six new ones were damaged. Nothing remained of the fence where the tree had landed, and an even larger section on the side was broken than they'd first thought.

Tori moved close and bumped shoulders with Kate. "Don't give up yet. It's not over just because a few things are broken."

"Tell that to my dad." Kate whispered the words, but she knew they were true. Dad stood with his arms crossed and a scowl darkening his usually happy face. This was definitely not good.

Mr. Jiménez and his wife tugged off their gloves and walked to Kate's parents. "We're sorry we can't stay longer," he said. "We're expecting company for lunch, and Mary needs to get home."

Dad nodded and pumped the man's hand. "We'll have you folks over for supper soon. If there's ever anything we can do to help you, please let us know. You've been a godsend today."

Mr. Jiménez motioned toward the remains of the trunk that still needed to come down. "I can help you take that down when you're ready, and I'll bring my log splitter over for the big pieces. Makes it a lot easier." He waved as he and his wife walked away.

Kate sidled close to her mother and tapped her arm. "Has Dad made a decision?" She tried to keep her voice low, but Tori's mother looked their way.

Dad swung around and faced the small group. "Nan, you'd better call the coordinator and tell her what happened. I don't see how we'll replace all of this in time for the show. Maybe they can find another location."

Mom hunched a shoulder. "I doubt it. She said it was a minor miracle they found us when they did. I'm guessing they'll have to cancel the show completely. It's a real shame, since it could have brought a lot of business to the barn, not to mention all the people who will be disappointed."

"Plus the ones, like Melissa, who won't be able to earn the points they need to move on to regionals." Kate couldn't keep from blurting out the information. After all, even though she didn't particularly like Melissa, she *was* one of their boarders.

Mom groaned. "I hadn't thought of that, but you're right, Kate. That's not going to go over well with a lot of people."

Dad frowned. "I can't see that we have any choice."

Kate cleared her throat. "Uh, can I make a suggestion?"

All eyes swung her way. "Go ahead," Dad said.

"You have money put aside to buy a lesson horse. Maybe we should use that to fix things instead—and you could use the money I have in savings too."

Mom's eyes lit with hope, then quickly dimmed. "No, I don't think so, but thank you for offering, honey. The show landed in our laps. We didn't ask for it. As nice as it would have been to host, we can't sacrifice the long-term investment of a lesson horse or your money in the hope that the show will make enough to pay that back."

Dad nodded. "I agree, although it was a sound idea, Kate." He jerked his head toward the house. "Nan, you probably had better call. No sense putting it off."

Tori's mom waved a hand. "May I make a suggestion?"

Mom smiled. "Of course. And we apologize. We should have waited to have this discussion until after you'd gone home."

"No, *mi amiga*, it's fine. Would you wait for an hour or two before you make that call?"

Dad frowned. "I'm not sure that's fair to the show coordinator."

Kate edged forward. "But it's not like they have somewhere else they can go, Dad. Would another hour or two hurt?"

He turned to Tori's mom. "Do you have a reason for asking?"

"I do, but may I wait to tell you? It may be nothing. In the meantime, shouldn't we ask God for direction in case He has another idea?"

The stern expression on Dad's face melted, and he looked a little sheepish. Kate wanted to giggle. He was usually the one telling their family they needed to talk to God about decisions. "I should have thought of that first. How about you folks come inside for coffee and cinnamon rolls?"

Tori's dad exchanged a glance with his wife, then shook his head. "May we take one or two to go?"

"Kate, Tori, would you girls run into the house and bring the plate out?"

Kate didn't wait to be asked again. She grabbed Tori's hand, and they raced across the edge of the pasture that separated the lawn from the arena. As soon as they were out of earshot, Kate leaned close to her friend. "What's up with your mom?"

"I have no idea." Tori turned wide eyes to Kate. "All I know is, we'd better take her advice and pray. Because if whatever it is doesn't happen, or God doesn't do something quick, this show is toast. At least that's the way your dad sounded."

Tori reached for the door and pulled it open, letting Kate go through first, then following. "But I have a feeling she's going to ask my dad if they can loan your parents the money. They've been saving for years to buy our own house."

Kate stared at Tori. "There's no way Mom and Dad would accept that. They won't take a chance with their own money for the lesson horse, so they're not going to risk yours."

"I know." Tori sounded defeated.

Kate walked through the living room to the kitchen and started piling cinnamon rolls on a plate. "And since money doesn't grow on trees like those branches did, I can't see any way we'll get all that stuff repaired and replaced in time. I think you're right. We'd better either pray for a miracle or get ready for a major disappointment."

Tori heaved a sigh and reached for a stack of napkins. "I vote for the miracle, but I hear what you're saying. Sometimes God answers no instead of yes, and we have to accept that, even if we're not happy with it."

Chapter Ten

Kate's dad put down the phone a couple of hours after Tori's family left. "I've never seen anything like this, Nan." He sank into a chair and stared at Kate's mom.

Kate scooted to the edge of the sofa, where she'd been watching TV without seeing it, not certain whether to be worried or hopeful. She couldn't tell much by her father's dazed expression. "What's going on, Dad? Was that Tori's mom or dad?"

Mom perched on the arm of the easy chair and rested her hand on his shoulder. "Good news, hon?"

His face broke into a smile. "Definitely good. That is, if we decide to accept. Mr. Velasquez called friends and neighbors, and Tori called the people who board at our barn. Apparently there are a few carpenters among the group, as well as an owner of a local building supply. No one wants to see the show canceled, as it brings a lot of business into the community. So tomorrow morning we're going to host what used to be called a barn raising, but in our case, it's an arena and jump building. Also, another barn has three jumps they're willing to lend us, so we won't have to build or repair as many right now."

Mom gasped. "Oh my goodness. I didn't hear much of the conversation, but did you tell them yes?"

He passed his palm over his chin. "I wasn't sure what to say. I told Mr. Velasquez that we were honored they'd want to do something like that, and it's an answer to prayer, but I needed to discuss it with you first."

Kate jumped to her feet. "What is there to discuss, Dad? If it's an answer to prayer, you should have thanked Tori's dad and said yes!"

Mom leveled a firm gaze at Kate. "I know you're excited, but you need to sit down. Let your father finish."

Kate scuffed her foot on the carpet, then sat. "I'm sorry, Dad."

Dad smiled. "Forgiven, sweetie. The reason I wanted to discuss it with you both first is because Mom will be in charge of putting together food for the work party. You and Tori can help, and Tori's mother offered too. But it's still going to be a big job. And I'll expect you to watch Pete as well. Think you can handle that?"

Kate's spirits sank a little. "I'd rather help outside."

"If we need extra help, I'll let you know. But you aren't a carpenter, and you can't handle a Skil saw or other power equipment. If there's a time your mom doesn't need you and Tori, you can be a gofer for the men."

She wrinkled her nose. "I'm not a rodent, Dad."

He laughed. "That means go for the things we need."

"Oh. Right. I can do that. I'm going to call Tori." She raced across the room, then halted and turned. "So are we doing this or not?" Kate looked at her mom.

Mom smiled. "I'm overwhelmed with the kindness of our friends and neighbors, and I'd love to cook and serve."

One more thought hit Kate. "Do you know if Melissa is coming?" She hoped not. It would be so much nicer to hang out with Tori and not have to deal with Melissa.

Dad nodded. "Tori's dad said most of the boarders had agreed to come, and I think she was one of them. Let me call Tori's dad back, then you can talk to Tori."

Kate left the room, her feet moving a bit slower than before. How silly to be bothered that Melissa had offered to work. She should be thankful for anyone who cared to come, but for some reason, she dreaded it. Kate perked up, though, when she thought of Colt. She'd need to call Colt and invite him. She'd have a ball with Colt and Tori, feeding people and doing anything they could to get ready for the show. What could possibly go wrong at a work party? After all, Melissa was one girl among a crowd of people, and Kate would simply keep her distance.

Kate raced to the front door the next morning, thankful Tori and her family had arrived before anyone else. Her mouth gaped at Tori's dad carrying two sacks of what appeared to be groceries. "Hey, you guys aren't supposed to bring food. It's enough that you're helping us." She ushered them into the house, then led the way to the kitchen, wishing her mother were here instead of upstairs getting Pete dressed.

Mr. Velasquez grinned and set the bags on the countertop. "*Si*, Maria insisted on the makings for tacos and fajitas, since several of our friends are coming. That way we'll have different types of dishes to choose from."

Tori bumped shoulders with Kate. "Yeah. Not just boring, old American food." She snickered and pulled a couple of filled quart jars out of a bag. "Mom's homemade spicy salsa. Yummy stuff. It'll burn the inside of your mouth if you're not careful."

Kate rolled her eyes. "So you're saying you don't want me able to talk, huh?"

Tori giggled. "Now *that* would be a change!"

"Hey!" Kate bumped her back, and they both burst out laughing. It felt good to laugh again, after the stress of the past couple of days. It was still hard to believe the arena and jumps would be rebuilt by nightfall. She sobered. "Thanks, Mr. and Mrs. Velasquez. Mom's going to be thrilled."

"With what, Kate?" Her mother's cheerful voice entered the room a second before she did. "Maria, I'm so glad you came!" She gave Mrs. Velasquez a hug.

Mr. Velasquez waved and headed for the door.

Kate drew her friend away as Tori's mom explained why she'd brought the groceries. Kate's mouth watered as she thought of the couple of times she'd eaten delicious Mexican food at Tori's house. She hoped there were leftovers.

"I called Colt," she explained to Tori. "He said he'd be here, and his dad might come too."

Tori's face lit up. "Cool!" She looked out the kitchen window toward the arena. "Cars are pulling in now. It's a good thing you have a big pasture area for parking. It'll come in handy for the show."

"I hope we can pull this off."

"What? Rebuilding everything?"

Kate shook her head. "Naw. I'm not worried about that. I mean the show. We've never done anything like this before. It feels … huge."

Tori crinkled her brows. "Like what? I don't follow."

"Hey, Mom," Kate called. "Do you need us, or can Tori and I go see what they're going to work on first?"

Her mother turned from examining the items in the grocery bags, then waved a distracted hand. "Scoot. Come back in an hour. We'll do the cooking, and you girls can serve. We're only serving coffee and snacks first. Later we'll have lunch."

"Thanks, Mom!" Kate grabbed Tori's hand and dashed out the door before her mother changed her mind. All it took to sidetrack her mom was a new recipe or another woman around who loved to cook, and she'd go off into her own world. It was a good thing Pete was watching a DVD in the living room, and Rufus was keeping him company.

Kate and Tori slowed halfway across the pasture. "So, to answer your question about the show…" Kate stopped and turned in a slow circle, pointing at the barn, the arena, and the parking area. "We'll have to get all of this cleaned up before people arrive, then set up the jumps for the outdoor arena, make room for the people who bring in concessions, separate pasture areas for horses, run power for the PA system, rope off areas for spectators to sit or stand, since we don't have bleachers. We'll even have people directing traffic for parking. And, of course, a company has to bring in porta-potties too. But the committee has already contacted someone for that."

Kate sighed. "It's going to be a madhouse with all those horse trailers and cars coming in the first hour or so, and some people have asked to come the night before and camp out. They asked the show coordinator if we have any paddocks or pens where they can keep their horses. Mom told them we have three large paddocks, so it won't be a problem. We'll use the outdoor arena for the classes."

"Wow! I had no idea. I guess I was envisioning a few classes with people handing out ribbons." Tori sucked in a breath. "So who comes up with the ribbons and the set of silver spurs?"

Kate grabbed Tori's arm and tugged her aside so a pickup loaded with miscellaneous pieces of lumber could pass, along with another car on its tail. People spilled out of both vehicles and headed toward the arena, some holding rakes, hammers, and other tools.

"The show committee provides all that—in fact, they have their own judges and even people who help with parking. The concession wagons all had to get permits and be approved in advance. I guess they pretty much go from show to show, so we don't have to mess with those either."

"Whew." Tori kicked a fir cone out of her path, then stooped and grabbed a broken branch. She swished it against her leg. "Sounds like most of it is under control."

"Except for all the prep work—getting pastures divided into pens, probably with temporary hot-wire tape. Then there's the cleanup. Dad wants to pressure-wash and paint the front doors of the barn, and Mom said the tack room and office need a good scrubbing. The time it's taking to do all the repairs to the fence and jumps is eating into the time we need to do all that other stuff now." Kate smiled. "Not that I'm complaining. It's a miracle your parents were able to round up so much help." She waved her hand toward the arena. "Let's go see what they plan to do first."

"I hope Colt gets here soon. Not that we can all hang out if we're working, but maybe we can hold boards while they nail them or paint the jumps when they're finished."

"Good plan. Let's ask Dad. I'm sure glad he was able to use a vacation day and get today off."

A few minutes later, Colt arrived with an older man Kate assumed was his father. Colt hurried to where the girls stood in the arena, as activity surged on all sides. Two men were manning a chop saw and cutting fence boards to length while two other men hammered them in place as soon as the boards were handed to them. Another group worked on the damaged jumps, while yet another, headed by a local contractor who attended Kate's church, started building new jumps to replace those damaged beyond repair.

Colt gazed from one spot to the next while his dad joined Kate's father. "So what can I do?"

Kate shrugged. "You could help cart out the big coffee urn the church loaned us and get it set up on a table."

"Sure. Where's the table?"

"Still in the house."

"What have you guys been doing?"

Kate shot Tori a sheepish glance. "Uh, not a whole lot, I'm afraid. Nothing is ready for paint yet, they don't trust us with a power saw or nail gun, and we're not very good with hammers."

Tori laughed. "So we've been going from one spot to the next telling everyone what a great job they're doing and trying not to get in the way."

Another car drove into the temporary parking area off to the side, and Melissa stepped out of the passenger side. She spotted Kate, Tori, and Colt, and lifted a hand, then moved their direction.

Pete ran up from the direction of the house and stopped by Tori. "You bring M&M's?"

Tori knelt beside Kate's little brother. "I'm sorry, buddy. I didn't think about it today."

Melissa covered the last several yards toward them, her face lit in a smile. "Hey, Pete, look what I brought." She held up a small bag of M&M's, then glanced at Kate. "It's okay to give him some, isn't it? He told me they're his favorite, so I made Dad stop at the store on the way."

Kate gaped at her, astounded not only at the caring reflected in Melissa's voice but at the thoughtful action on Pete's behalf. "As long as you don't give them all to him. We'll have lunch in an hour or so, and Mom won't want him to have too much sugar before then."

"Sure. No problem." She held out her hand to Pete. "Want to hang out with me for a while, Pete? We can eat M&M's and pick up a few loose branches and put them in the burn pile. Would that be fun?"

The boy didn't look at her, but he extended his hand and allowed her to take his. Kate could see his fingers were almost limp, but just the same, she was shocked that he'd allowed Melissa to touch him. "Rufus too?" He patted his leg with his other hand, and the big shepherd bounded over, tongue lolling. Sidling up to Melissa, the dog stuck his nose in her hand. She stuffed the bag of M&M's in her pocket, then stroked his ears and patted his head. "You aren't such a bad boy, are you?"

Melissa arched her brows at Kate, Tori, and Colt but didn't smile. "Let me know if you need anything else done. Until then, I'll keep Pete company."

Kate nodded dumbly. "Sure. Okay. Thanks." She watched them walk away, Melissa leaning over to place an M&M in Pete's hand as they went. "I don't get it." Kate kept her voice low, but she wanted to scream. Her own dog and her brother! Even after Melissa had chased Rufus with a rope and smacked him. What a traitor. She didn't mind Rufus coming to Pete, but he could have at least growled at Melissa.

Tori narrowed her eyes. "What?"

"How she can be so nice to Pete and so rude to us sometimes. It's almost like there's two different people trapped inside her body, and they're both fighting to get out."

Colt nodded. "I saw her be wicked to people at the other barn. Then she'd turn around and surprise me by doing something kind. I wonder if there's anything going on in her life that she keeps hidden. Know what I mean?"

"I suppose it's possible, but from what I can tell, she's privileged, her family has money, and she doesn't have a care in the world. The horse she rides must have cost thousands." Kate exhaled. "I want to know how she gets through to Pete like that. He holds my mom's hand sometimes, but not very often. It's like Melissa's cast some kind of spell over him."

"You should be happy your little brother is responding to anyone, even if it's Melissa," Tori scoffed. "Besides, no one can be all bad and have kids and dogs take to them."

"Yeah, but that's the problem. She screamed at Rufus and chased him. He shouldn't have let her pet him."

Colt chuckled. "He came because Pete called him. Maybe he smelled the M&M's on Melissa's hand and hoped he'd get a taste."

"Right." Kate tried not to grumble, but she could barely muster a smile. If things kept going this way, everyone would be in love with Melissa.

Chapter Eleven

Three days after the workday, Kate and Tori stared as the doors on the rented horse trailer were opened. Kate squeezed Tori's hand. "Can you believe he's finally here? Our very own lesson horse!"

Stars shone in Tori's eyes as she looked from Kate to the gray horse backing out of the trailer. "It's so cool your parents were able to get him. I can't believe someone traded him for full board. I can take a few lessons on him before the show. I'm not sure I'll be ready for a beginner's walk-trot class, but I've decided to try if Mrs. Jamison thinks I am."

"Awesome! The people who owned Mr. Gray said he's a sweet, kind horse. They would have kept him, but their daughter wants to show on the circuit, and he's too old to compete at the level she's hoping for. He's trained at flat work as well as beginner jumping."

Tori hugged herself and shivered. "I'm so excited! Is he a Thoroughbred?"

"No, he's an Appendix. The owner said that means he's part Quarter horse and part Thoroughbred, so he has a little spunk, but he's not an airhead. He's very steady."

"Good. I don't want to fall off again."

Kate grabbed Tori's hand. "Let's go give him some carrots and make friends."

The next day Kate stood by Colt on the sidelines of the arena as Tori stepped into Mr. Gray's stirrup. Tori's hands shook as she picked up the reins. Mrs. Jamison smiled and patted Tori's leg. "Don't worry. I rode Mr. Gray this morning, and he's a doll. He listened to everything, whether you use your hands, voice, or legs, and he never once tried to take advantage."

Tori grimaced. "But you aren't a beginner. He knows he has to behave for you."

Mrs. Jamison walked to the center of the ring. "You've ridden enough that you're not a brand-new beginner either. You're better than you think, Tori. You simply need a boost of confidence. Now gather the reins until you have light contact with his mouth the way I showed you, and barely touch him with your heel."

Tori did as she was instructed, her face screwed into a deep well of concentration. Mr. Gray moved out immediately, ambling down the rail.

"All right, good. Now a very light squeeze with your calves. He can walk faster than that."

"But I don't want to trot yet." Tori gripped the reins tighter.

"We're not asking him to trot. Do as I ask, and you'll be fine."

Kate couldn't even see Tori's legs move, but the gray horse lengthened his stride and moved into a fast walk. Kate beamed at Colt and leaned close to whisper. "She did it!"

Colt grinned in return. "Yeah. She needs to get over her nerves, and she'll be fine."

Kate's smile faded as realization hit. "It's my fault that she's scared. She's never gotten over the fall she took off Capri. That was one of the dumbest things I've ever done."

"Ah, you need to quit worrying about it. All you can do is learn from it and not do it again." He waved toward the arena. "I'll guarantee she gets past her fear today after riding this horse. Your parents found a good one."

"I think so too." She rested her arms on the rail overlooking the arena. "So are you entering the show? They're offering a few Western classes, so you won't have to dress up in breeches." She snickered and ducked when he tried to swat her. "Ha. You missed!"

Colt pointed to the ring. "I heard Mrs. Jamison say some- .
thing about trotting. Think Tori will go for it?"

"She trotted Lulu several times, but this horse is bigger, and
she isn't used to him. I'm not sure."

Mrs. Jamison took three strides toward the walking gelding,
keeping pace with him as he traveled along the rail. "Do you
understand posting, Tori?"

"I think so, but I'm not very good at it."

"Let the motion of the horse's stride help push you up. Rise
as his front inside leg goes forward and sit as his outside leg, the
one closest to the rail, moves forward. Don't push off your feet.
Grip with your thighs and push up from there."

"You mean I have to trot?"

"Yes. You have very quiet hands, Tori, and a good seat.
There's no reason you can't trot that horse. Don't post the first
circle if you're worried. When you're ready, kiss to him and
lightly squeeze him with your calves. Very lightly, though, so he
doesn't go into a canter."

Tori made a kissing sound, but nothing happened. Mr. Gray
continued to walk.

"Did you use your legs?"

Tori bit her lip. "I was worried he'd canter."

"You'd have to give him a harder bump for that. Kiss and try
squeezing harder with your calves instead. He should respond."

Tori repeated the process, and the gelding moved into a smooth trot. "Oh! He's doing it!"

"How does he feel?"

"Much easier to sit than Lulu. She was choppy."

"That's the pony you took lessons on? They're always choppy because they have short legs and a short stride. Mr. Gray's legs are much longer, and he's more fluid in the way he travels. Keep light contact with his mouth, and make a full circle. Then I want you to try posting. Don't stress if it's not perfect or even on the correct lead. Just rise and fall to his stride." She waited several seconds, then nodded. "Good girl. You're getting it. Later we'll need to work on rising with his inside leg, but you've got the right idea."

Kate heaved a huge sigh of relief. She'd actually seen Tori smile. It appeared her friend might have conquered her fear. If only she'd be willing to enter at least one class in the show, life would be perfect.

Capri nickered from her stall as though she'd been forgotten. Kate moved from the rail and walked a couple of yards to her mare's stall. "Hey, girl, here's a carrot." She dug one out of her pocket and slipped it through the bars. "You're going to be the champion at the show, I know it. Maybe I'll even win the silver spurs. If any horse here can do it, it's you."

Colt moved up beside her. "Dreaming about the show?"

Kate felt heat rise into her cheeks, and she ducked her head. "Yeah, I guess. Kind of. I've wanted to compete for the longest time. I wish I could have had jumping lessons and entered some of the hunter classes. I guess this time around I'll have to be happy with the flat classes."

Colt nodded. "That's all I'll ever enter, since it doesn't work too well to jump in a Western saddle. I've thought about competitive trail riding, but it's not that important to me. Honestly, I'd rather hit the real trails any day than ride around in circles in a ring all the time."

"I've never gotten to do much trail riding," Kate admitted. "Mom worries about the traffic on the roads, even though we're not close to town."

"Maybe someday we can put together a trail ride up toward Mount Hood. Did you know there are horse corrals up there and tons of riding trails?"

"Cool! That would be a blast as long as we didn't get lost."

"That's why you have a guide or take someone with you who knows the area. I imagine you could get off on a trail and lose your way if you weren't careful … So back to the show. Have you heard if Melissa is entering Mocha in the jumping classes? She might be the best chance for your barn to win the silver spurs."

Anger sparked in Kate. "Why does that matter? It's not like Melissa is riding a horse that we own or anything."

"No, but she boards and takes lessons here. It can't do any harm if she won, that's for sure." He leaned against the wall next to Capri's stall.

Kate moved back to the rail and fixed her gaze on Tori, wishing Colt would go home. Why did things always have to come back to Melissa and ruin everything she'd dreamed about? Sure, Melissa had a well-trained, expensive horse, but Capri had some awesome training as well. And it wasn't going to be long before Kate could keep up with the other girl. All she needed was a few jumping classes, and she'd prove to her friends that she was every bit as good as Melissa.

Chapter Twelve

Kate jumped out of bed the morning of the show and hurried to the window, praying the rain shower had stopped. She'd lain in bed late last night listening to it patter against the eaves, certain it would ruin the show. Shoving aside the curtains in her second-floor room, she pumped a fist in the air. "Yes! Sun!"

She whirled around the room in a circle, landing on her bed. The weather wouldn't ruin the show after all. She was grateful that God had listened to her prayers last night and that her lack of faith hadn't gotten in His way.

Scrambling for her jeans and T-shirt, she gathered them from a pile on the floor and tugged them on as fast as possible. She'd put clean clothes on later, but right now her top priority was to get downstairs, have breakfast, and see what she could do to help.

Excitement and fear battled inside. Her first horse show. She'd gotten to attend one before, but never to compete. What would it be like? Would she get so scared when she rode Capri into the ring that she'd throw up or pass out? Now that would be embarrassing. She giggled, suddenly seeing a picture of herself keeling over before she had a chance to climb into the saddle. Nope. Wasn't gonna happen.

Kate slowed her rush down the stairs as another thought hit. How about Tori? If Kate's nerves had nailed her, how would her best friend be feeling? She didn't have any experience at all. She'd never even been to a show. Colt was lucky. He'd attended several shows and competed more than once, so this would probably be a cinch for him.

Good thing she'd been able to take several lessons over the last few weeks so she felt more confident about taking classes. She'd have to stick close to Tori and help all she could, reassuring her if she got too scared or wanted to chicken out—that couldn't happen. They were in this together, and it was going to be fun!

Kate raced into the kitchen, then skidded to a halt. Pete sat at the table eating a bowl of cold cereal. His favorite. He rarely ate eggs or toast or pancakes. She shook her head and smiled. In some ways, it was kind of nice to have things she could depend on. She walked behind Pete and ruffled his hair. As usual, he ducked his head and mumbled. But he didn't pull away as much as he usually did, so that was something. "Hi, buddy. Good cereal?"

He nodded, and Kate's heart skipped. Another good sign. Maybe he was excited about the show as well. "You going to hang out with Dad and watch the horse show today?"

Pete dipped his spoon in the cereal and carefully lifted it to his mouth, but he didn't respond. Kate squatted by his chair and touched his arm. For once he didn't flinch, but he didn't seem to notice her presence. The spoon went into the bowl again and back to his parted lips. No show of emotion at all. She rocked back on her heels, struggling to push down her disappointment. What had she expected? For him to grin and tell her how much he was looking forward to the show?

Mom stood by the stove stirring something in a pan. She put the spatula down and took a step toward Kate, then gently set a hand on her shoulder. "Baby steps, Kate. Baby steps. Don't expect too much. Take it one day at a time, okay?"

Kate heaved a soft sigh before pushing to her feet. "Yeah. Right. It's just hard sometimes."

Her mother gave her a quick hug, then moved back to the stove. "I know. But if it wasn't hard, it would mean you didn't care." She gestured toward the cupboard. "Get out three plates, silverware, glasses, and orange juice. Dad will be inside in a minute, and these scrambled eggs are hot." She pushed the lever on the toaster, and four slices disappeared inside.

Kate hurried to complete the task and looked up as her father entered through the kitchen door. "Hey, Dad, everything okay at the barn?"

"Yep. Your mother and I got up early and fed the horses so we can spend the next hour getting the jumps set up in the outdoor arena. People will start arriving by eight o'clock, and we need to be ready."

"Thanks, Dad. That's great. I thought getting up at five would give us plenty of time. I hope Tori and Colt get here soon."

Her father slid out his chair. When he, Kate, and her mother were all seated, he smiled at Pete. "We're going to pray, Pete. Can you join us?"

Pete stared around the table, not meeting anyone's eyes, but he seemed more focused than Kate had seen him in a while. He nodded. "Pete will pray."

Kate froze, afraid if she moved or said anything, it would ruin everything.

Dad bowed his head, as though nothing special had happened. "Sure, Pete. Go ahead and talk to Jesus for us."

Kate kept her eyes open, fascinated by this new turn of events.

Pete ignored her and their parents. He lifted his eyes to the ceiling. "God? Help us all be happy and good. Amen." Then he picked up his spoon and dipped it into the cereal again as though he hadn't done anything extraordinary.

Mom raised her eyes from where she sat across the table from Kate, and tears trickled down her cheeks. She offered a wavering smile. "Amen." She sucked in a quick breath. "Now we'd better hurry and eat so we can get outside before the early birds arrive and throw us all into a tizzy!" She laughed and wiped her damp cheeks, then picked up her fork and dug into her fluffy scrambled eggs.

After breakfast, Kate slipped over to stand beside her mother at the dishwasher. "Pete has never offered to pray before."

Mom gave a radiant smile. "I know. It was amazing."

Kate nodded. "I never told you, but he did something else that was unusual the day everyone came over to help rebuild the arena and the jumps. He took Melissa's hand when she offered it."

"That is unusual, especially with someone who's almost a stranger."

"Melissa has worked to get to know Pete since she's been boarding here."

"That's very kind."

"Yeah." Kate hesitated, wondering how much of her concern to share. "I don't get her. She's nice to Pete, and sometimes she's even decent to me and Colt and Tori. Other times she acts like the Wicked Witch of the West who thinks we're her minions."

Mom laughed and ruffled Kate's hair. "Don't let her bother you. She's one of our boarders, so we'll be courteous, regardless. You never know what's in a person's heart or what might be going on behind the scenes. Now we'd better get a move on."

Two hours later Kate and Tori slipped into the barn wearing their riding breeches, white shirts, and boots. Kate wished they'd been able to afford real leather boots, but at least she had a complete outfit, even if it was used. At this point she was thankful they'd found an English store in Portland that carried a selection of nice-quality clothing and equipment on consignment, and both she and Tori were able to get outfitted at a reasonable cost.

Pretty much everything was done, and Kate released a sigh. She was too keyed up to be tired, even if she'd been up for three hours, and it was only eight o'clock in the morning. The first class would start in an hour, and both she and Tori needed to groom their horses and make sure all their tack was in order. She elbowed Tori as they walked down the alleyway. "Aren't you excited? It's our first show, and we both get to compete."

Tori rubbed her belly. "I'm not sure if I'm excited or sick, but my stomach feels like it's going to heave."

Kate slipped her arm through Tori's. "You're nervous. It will all go away as soon as you ride into the ring. I'll bet it's the same as walking onto a stage when you're in a play. You say your opening line and voilà! Everything is back to normal, and the show goes on."

"Yeah. Or you stand there and faint or hurl all over the stage."

"Hmm." Kate swung Tori around and gazed at her. "This is the first time you're pastier than me, and I've got pale skin. Shake it off, girl. It's not like you're going in front of a firing squad."

"Feels like it." Tori groaned and pressed her hands into her abdomen. "Seriously, I'm not sure I'll get through this without being sick."

Kate tugged her forward. "Come on. You'll forget all about it as soon as you start grooming Mr. Gray. Hasn't it been fun riding him? I can't believe how much you've improved! You know how to post now and everything."

"I'm glad I'm only entering the walk-trot class for beginners. I don't think I could handle any more than that."

They continued down the alleyway. Suddenly Mocha's stall door slid open, and Melissa catapulted out, almost running into Kate. "There you are. I was coming to find you."

Kate took a step back. "What's up?" She didn't care for Melissa's scowl or the brittleness of her tone.

"I'm in several classes today, and the person who usually grooms for me and changes tack can't come. I need you to take care of that for me."

Kate crossed her arms over her chest. "Sorry. No can do."

Melissa seemed to look at Kate for the first time. "Why are you in riding gear? You and your parents run this place. Shouldn't you be taking care of your customers?"

Kate almost had to bite her tongue to keep from saying something she'd regret. Only her mother's warning that morning about being kind to their customers reined in her temper. "We're competing in classes too. And no, it's not our job to take care of our boarders today. This is a horse show that happens to be held at our barn. We're hosting it, not putting it on. We're as free to take part as anyone else."

"So who's going to help me?" Melissa's voice dropped to a low rumble. "I *have* to win those silver spurs, and I think you're being mean not to agree."

Kate couldn't keep a lid on her emotions any longer. "Well, *sor-ry!*" She grabbed Tori's hand, and they continued down the alleyway to Capri's stall. "She's got some nerve!" she hissed close to Tori's ear. "Who does she think she is? And why did she say she *has* to win the spurs?"

"Dunno. Pretty weird, if you ask me." Tori slapped her forehead. "We didn't grab the grooming box for Capri. Guess we'll have to make a dash to the tack room and hope she doesn't see us."

"Ugh." Kate grunted and leaned against the inside of the stall as Capri munched hay from the feeder in the corner. "I wish I never had to see that girl again."

Chapter Thirteen

Kate stood at the rail of the indoor arena, holding her breath as Tori rode by on Mr. Gray. Her friend's face hadn't gained much more color than earlier, but at least she hadn't fainted or hurled. Kate nudged Colt in the side with her elbow. "She's doing great, huh?"

He kept his gaze fixed on Tori as she and Mr. Gray moved down the rail on the far side of the arena. "Yeah. And it's a bigger class than I expected. I didn't realize there were eight kids under the age of eighteen who would qualify for a walk-trot class." He tilted his head toward a girl as she rode by on a sorrel mare. "I'm almost positive she doesn't belong in there, though."

Kate arched a brow. "Why not?"

"You're supposed to be a novice for this class, which means you've never placed in a show. I think she took a fifth-place ribbon at a show in The Dalles—I'm not sure, but her name sounds familiar."

"Should we say something?"

"Not unless she wins, and even then, I'm not sure it's our place. It happens sometimes, although that doesn't make it right."

Indignation stiffened Kate's spine. "No kidding! If she does win, I'll mention it to my mom. And maybe to Mrs. Jamison."

Colt nodded but kept watching Tori. "She's doing good. I can't believe how much better she's gotten since she started riding your lesson horse."

"She says it's all Mr. Gray, but I told her she only needed a little bit of confidence to bring out the good rider inside. He's a super horse, and we're lucky we got him."

Static from the loudspeaker crackled a second before the announcer's voice boomed. "Walk your horses, please. Walk your horses."

Everyone in the ring slowed to a walk and continued around the circle. Tori kept light pressure on the reins, and Mr. Gray kept his nose down and walked at a steady pace. Kate noticed that the girl Colt had pointed out couldn't seem to keep her horse from breaking into a trot. Served her right if she was trying to cheat by entering a class she didn't qualify for.

As the girl rode past, Kate saw tears glinting on the girl's cheeks, and remorse hit her. What if the girl, who wasn't any older than Tori, didn't know the rules or thought she had to place first in another class to be disqualified for this one? *Maybe Dad's right. He says sometimes I'm too hasty to judge.* Kate almost hoped the girl would win a ribbon, even if it was fifth again.

"Line up, please. Everyone line up in the center of the ring," the announcer boomed again, making Kate jump. Everything echoed in here, and she was surprised it hadn't spooked any horses.

The eight horses and riders formed a straight line across the center of the arena, and a judge walked into the ring. She stopped in front of each one, asking the rider to back the horse a few steps, then move forward and halt. Kate heaved a huge sigh after Mr. Gray executed his command perfectly.

Only minutes later, the loudspeaker crackled as a young girl walked into the arena holding a handful of brightly colored ribbons. "As I call your name, please walk your horse forward and accept your ribbon. Then you may exit the ring."

Colt nudged Kate. "What do you think? Does Tori have a chance?"

Kate nodded. "I'm no judge, but I think so. A couple of the other riders did really well too, but Tori looked great."

"Fifth place goes to Myra Robbins from The Dalles." The girl who'd been crying rode forward and accepted her ribbon, her somber face breaking into a smile.

Colt grunted. "Think we should say something?"

"Naw. Let it go. If someone in the class knows she doesn't belong there, they can bring it up."

"Right. Good call."

"Fourth place goes to Ryan Smith from White Salmon, Washington."

"A dude?" Colt shook his head. "I was watching Tori and the other girl so much, I didn't catch that."

"Lots of guys ride English." Kate smirked at him. "You should try it, Colt."

"Not on your life."

"Third place goes to Marcy Kingston from Mosier, Oregon."

Kate clutched Colt's arm. "There are two places left and five people. I'm so nervous for Tori!"

"Yeah."

A rustle of papers sounded over the speaker. "Second place goes to Tori Velasquez from Odell."

Kate squealed and clapped her hands, and Colt pumped his fist in the air. "Way to go, Tori!"

Tori rode forward and accepted her red ribbon as color flooded her face. Kate and Colt rushed around to the gate at the end of the arena, not even caring to hear who won first place. As far as Kate was concerned, Tori was a champion!

As soon as Tori cleared the gate, she dismounted. Kate swooped in and grabbed her in a hug, squealing the entire time.

Colt took Mr. Gray's reins and patted Tori's shoulder. "Way to go, squirt. You did good."

Tori gazed at both of them with glazed eyes. "I can't believe it." She held up the ribbon, then swung around as her mother rushed up and enveloped her in a hug. "Mom? Did you see my class?"

"*Si*, silly goose. I was across the arena from Kate and Colt, cheering for you. I'm so proud of you, *mi hija*."

Tori grinned at them before focusing her attention on Kate. "Now it's Kate's turn, and Colt's."

Colt scuffed his boot on the ground. "I decided to scratch my one class."

"What?" a chorus of voices echoed. "Why?" Kate glared at her friend, hardly able to believe what he'd said.

"It was only one class, and I wasn't crazy about Western Equitation. Besides, I saw Melissa earlier, and she needs help, so I told her I'd groom her horse between classes."

Kate stared, trying to absorb what he'd said. "She was rude to Tori and me earlier. Why would you do that, Colt?"

"Why not? It's not like I don't have time."

Tori narrowed her eyes. "Are you crushing on her?"

Colt blew out a hard breath. "No way! I kind of feel sorry for her."

"You wouldn't if she'd talked to you like she did to us," Kate said.

Mrs. Velasquez patted Colt's arm. "I'm proud of you for doing the right thing, even if she isn't a nice girl." She turned to Tori. "Want me to take care of your ribbon so you can help Kate get ready for her class?"

"Sure, thanks, Mom." Tori handed the red rosette over and linked arms with Kate. "Come on. Your turn to wow the crowd."

All of a sudden, Kate's pulse sped up. Wow the crowd? She didn't expect to do any such thing. Would she live up to Tori's second place or maybe earn a first? She hadn't thought past entering a class and having fun. Now she knew what Tori felt like an hour ago. "I have time. I want to go outside and watch one of the jumping classes first. Okay with you guys?"

"Sure." Tori nodded. "You coming, Colt?"

He shook his head. "Melissa's got a class coming up soon. I need to get Mocha ready."

"What's she doing? Can't she get her own horse ready?" Kate frowned.

"She can, but it's hard when you've got your best clothes on, and the horse has to be cooled and groomed and tacked up between classes. It's a lot easier if you only have one or two classes, and they're further apart."

Shame tugged at Kate. "I never thought of that. I assumed she wanted a slave to take care of her because she thought she was too good to do it herself."

Tori hung her head. "Yeah, me too."

Tori's confession made Kate feel a little better, but she still shouldn't have gotten so angry when Melissa asked for help. Then a memory hit her. Melissa hadn't *asked* them, she'd *demanded*, even making that weird comment about having to win the spurs. What was that about anyway? Kate raised her hand. "Have fun, Colt. And tell Melissa I hope she does well in her next class. Any idea how she did in her first one?"

"She got a first in English Equitation. She's pretty solid when it comes to her skills. She's hoping Mocha will do as well in English Pleasure, but it's the jumping class later today she's hoping to ace." He waved and pivoted. "See you later. I'll be sure and watch your class, Kate."

"Thanks."

What was up with him and Melissa? He'd made it clear he didn't want Melissa as a girlfriend, and Kate believed him. Colt was a really nice guy. Maybe he simply wanted to help someone who was having a struggle, as he claimed. Whatever it was, she was glad she wasn't the one helping Melissa. Somehow Kate guessed the girl would be hard to please and strung as tight as a finely tuned guitar string.

Kate, Tori, and Colt sat outside on the grass, waiting for the first jumping class to begin. Colt had finished grooming and tacking up Mocha, and Melissa had headed for the arena without a word to Kate or Tori as she passed. Kate wasn't surprised. As Kate's grandmother always said, she'd seen the handwriting on the wall.

Kate turned to Colt. "Did she thank you for helping?"

He lounged on his elbows, a long blade of grass between his lips. "Yeah. Kind of, I guess. I think she's more nervous about the next couple of classes than Tori was about hers."

Tori rolled her eyes. "Right. Melissa is the queen of cool. Nothing shakes her."

"Not what I saw a few minutes ago."

"What's up with her?" Kate had felt her own batch of butterflies dancing in her belly over her upcoming class, but now wasn't the time to admit it. She was more interested in hearing what Colt thought about Melissa.

"Dunno. She didn't say much. Really uptight. Not sure what's going on."

The first rider entered the arena, and all three of them sat up and leaned forward. This was the most exciting part of the show—jumping—at least as far as Kate was concerned. Part of her hoped Melissa would do well, but the ornery part of her wished she'd get taken down a notch or two. Maybe she'd quit being so snotty if she didn't always win.

Tori rested her elbows on her knees. "So is this a superhard course or an easy one? I'm clueless."

Colt looked at Kate. She smiled and said, "It's an easy one. Low jumps and placed far enough apart to give the horse and rider time to recover. No water jumps, nothing terribly hard. It's more for beginner to intermediate riders."

After the third horse exited the ring, Kate shook her head. "Only one clean round so far."

"Nuh-uh." Tori wrinkled her nose. "Three horses have gone over all the jumps without knocking down a single bar."

"Yeah, I know," Kate said. "But two of them were slow and didn't do it within the time allowed, so they got time faults. That's as bad as knocking down a bar. They were being careful—but too careful."

Colt shushed them. "Melissa and Mocha just came into the ring."

"He's gorgeous." Tori breathed the words with a reverent tone. "Funny. I never used to notice horses."

All three of them stood and edged closer to the fence, trying not to get in anyone's way. They found a spot near the corner with an excellent view of the final run of jumps. Melissa cantered around the inside perimeter of the arena, then reined Mocha toward the first jump. As he got within two or three strides, she slowed his pace. The big horse gathered himself and

launched over the obstacle without hesitation, landing grace-
fully on the other side.

Tori clapped and bounced on her toes. "He makes it look
so easy! And he doesn't care about the flags waving on the stan-
dards or anything."

Kate kept her eyes trained on the gelding. "He's rushing the
next fence. He's going too fast. Melissa needs to slow him down ..."

She felt Tori's grip on her arm as Melissa tightened her
hold on the big horse and brought him under control at the
last second. He shortened his stride in time to adjust and clear
the bar, skimming the pole but not knocking it down. Kate
released her breath in a whoosh. "Wow. That was close."

The rest of the round, Melissa kept a tight rein on Mocha
but cut a few corners to make up time. She finished with a
clean round, with under two seconds before the clock ran out.
She patted her horse's neck as he trotted toward the exit, then
pulled him to a stop and jumped to the ground.

"What's wrong? What's she doing?" Tori craned her neck
trying to see what had caused the unusual action.

Kate shook her head. "I'm not sure. She's running her hand
down over his cannon bone."

"What's that?"

Colt pointed. "The long, slender bone between his
knee and his fetlock—you might think of the fetlock as his

ankle joint. She must be worried he injured himself on the course."

Melissa straightened, and Kate saw fear flash across her expression before she turned away and led Mocha out of the arena.

"He's limping," Colt said. "Not good at all. He still has the biggest course later this afternoon. Melissa won't stand a chance of winning the championship if she can't enter that class."

Chapter Fourteen

Kate and her friends lingered outside the barn, hoping for word on Melissa's horse. "How long will the vet take to examine him? I'd think he'd be finished by now." Kate turned to Colt. "You said you want to be a vet someday. Do you know what he's doing?"

"I volunteer, but so far I've mostly cleaned kennels and walked dogs at the clinic. I imagine he's checking Mocha's tendons and maybe doing X-rays of his bone."

"Seriously?" Kate hadn't expected something like that.

"Yeah. They have portable X-ray machines, and it's not a big deal to bring one out. I hope Mocha's okay."

"Me too." Kate whispered the words, regretting she'd wished that Melissa would lose. She didn't even know how many points she'd gotten or what her standing was in the class because they'd all been hanging around the barn since the injury.

A couple of minutes later, Kate's mom waved at them and walked over. "Mocha might have bowed a tendon. The vet isn't sure. Or it could be something as simple as popping a splint on his bone, and if so, that will heal in time and won't cause permanent injury."

Kate closed her eyes and sighed. "So that's good, right? I mean, if it's a splint instead of a tendon? How soon can she ride him again? Any chance he'll be okay by the time Melissa needs to enter the final class?"

"No. The vet wrapped his leg and iced it, but she has instructions not to use Mocha for the next month."

Tori cringed. "What a bummer for Melissa."

Her mother nodded. "Hadn't you better get ready for your class, Kate? You've been waiting for this for a long time."

"Yeah," she mumbled. But somehow her heart wasn't in it. She felt terrible for Melissa. She could only imagine what she'd be going through if it had happened to Capri.

Colt patted his stomach. "I'm starving. You guys got everything under control, or do you need help?"

Kate waved her hand. "Go eat. You're looking awfully skinny. Tori and I can take care of things."

"Fine." He grinned at them both. "Want me to bring you something?"

"Naw. I'm not going to eat till my class is over."

"Scared?" He quirked a smile.

"No way. I just don't want to spill any food on my clothes, that's all."

"Right." He winked, then sauntered off, a cheerful whistle drifting after him.

Tori nudged Kate's arm. "So, you're nervous too, huh? You didn't want Colt to know 'cause he'd tease you?"

Kate shrugged. "I guess. Mostly, though, I'm worried about Melissa and don't feel like eating. She's got to be so upset."

"Maybe we should stop by her stall and tell her we're sorry."

Kate perked up. "Good plan. Let's go."

She was thankful most of the indoor classes were finished for now, and the afternoon ones wouldn't start for another hour. Most of the spectators and participants were outside watching the final round of jumps before lunch. She had more than enough time to get Capri groomed and her tack checked out before her class.

They neared Mocha's stall and slowed their pace. "Do you suppose the vet is gone? We don't want to barge in if Melissa's still busy," Kate whispered.

"Right. Let's hang here for a minute and see if we hear anything." Tori stopped near the door two stalls down and leaned against the wall.

Kate slid the door open, thankful the stall was empty, and beckoned Tori inside. She dropped her voice. "In case the vet comes out, we don't want him or Melissa to think we're spying on them. If he walks by, we'll wait a minute or two and then go, casual like, and tell her we're sorry about what happened."

Tori nodded, her eyes wide.

Footsteps approached from the opposite direction. They didn't come from Mocha's stall, but from the way it sounded they stopped right in front of it.

"Mom!" Melissa's voice rang through the walls separating them.

"Melissa. I got here hoping to see your first jumping class, and I was directed here. I passed the vet in the parking lot, and he told me Mocha will be fine. What's going on?"

Kate and Tori looked at each other, and Tori leaned in close to murmur, "Should we try to escape?"

"I'm afraid they'd see or hear us," Kate whispered back. "Let's hang here for now until they leave. We'll catch up with Melissa later, since her mom's with her."

Melissa's voice was low, but her words carried through to the empty stall. "Mocha can't finish the show."

"What? But the vet said he'd be fine."

"He will, with proper rest and care. I can't use him for at least a month. I'm sorry, Mom."

Kate arched her brows at Tori. Why should Melissa tell her mother she was sorry Mocha got hurt, as if it was something that would upset her mom more than Melissa? Weird. Kate held perfectly still, hating to eavesdrop but intrigued in spite of herself.

Melissa's mother's voice went up a notch. "That is not acceptable, Melissa. You *must* finish your classes today. You've taken a first in one class. How about this last one?"

"I haven't heard, but I made it with no penalty points, so I imagine I'll place, even if I don't get first place."

Something that sounded like a hand hitting the wall made Kate and Tori jump. "You need a first or a second in every class to make regionals."

"I know that." A note of desperation had crept into Melissa's voice. "But what am I supposed to do? He's lame. I can't ride him. It's over."

"It can't be over!" Melissa's mother said in an icy tone. "My standing at the country club is based on your success as a rider … and your father's money. I can't keep up this charade much longer. Finances are tight. We *need* this win, Melissa." There was a slight pause, and her tone turned condescending. "Your prestige among your peers hinges on this win too—as well as your dream to make the Olympic team someday. Then there are college scholarships. This win would ensure you getting into regionals."

Kate and Tori, shocked, stared at each other.

"So are you going to pull another horse out of a hat, then?" Sarcasm and fear dripped from Melissa's voice. A sharp slap echoed through the stall. "Mom! I can't believe you hit me!"

"I will not tolerate disrespect, Melissa. Not from you or anyone else. How about the lesson horse at this barn? Can't you use him?"

Tori stiffened next to Kate, and they shot each other a look.

"He's not a high enough level, from what I've heard. He's mostly used for flat work and low jumps—hunter-jumper, not intermediate or advanced jumping. Besides, I haven't taken lessons on him, so I doubt Mrs. Ferris would allow me to use him."

"We'll see about that."

"No! Mom, I told you. He can't compete at the level I need for my final class. He'd fail going over the jumps. Would you rather I scratch the class or look foolish riding a horse that's obviously not up to it?"

Mrs. Tolbert heaved a deep sigh. "Neither. I want you to ride in that class and win. But I'm beginning to see that might not be a viable option."

"Exactly." Melissa sounded on the verge of tears, and Kate's heart twisted.

"I am not happy about this, Melissa. But I believe I have a solution."

Silence followed her declaration. Kate and Tori exchanged glances and took a step closer to the wall.

"Fine. If you're just going to stand there and stare at me, I'll tell you. I'm going to contact the vet and tell him to give Mocha a heavy painkiller so you can ride him in the final class. Since the vet said he'll be fine with a bit of rest, I can't imagine a ten-minute ride will hurt."

Melissa gasped. "No way! The vet will never agree, and I won't either. I love that horse, and I'm not going to risk crippling him."

"That's absurd. So ride him, then let him take five weeks off instead of a month, but I doubt that will be necessary, with the proper medication. Why, anything is possible with drugs."

"I will not ride him, Mom."

"You'll do as you're told, and that's final." The stall door slid open.

Footsteps receded in the opposite direction, and Kate wilted against the interior stall wall. She beckoned for Tori to come close and put her lips against her ear. "Let's get out of here."

Tori's eyes turned toward the stall where Melissa must still have been with her horse.

Sobs that had barely been discernible suddenly escalated into a full-throated cry. Kate grabbed Tori's hand and slid the door open, then both girls tiptoed toward the closest exit.

Kate could barely concentrate on her class as she entered the ring. Melissa's sobs still rang in her ears. How could her mother threaten to have her horse drugged so she could compete? She shuddered and patted Capri's neck, thankful neither of her parents was so focused on winning that they'd do something underhanded and hurtful.

The announcer gave the command to trot, and Kate concentrated on rising on the correct diagonal. She could do this in her sleep now, but apparently not with Melissa on her mind. She and Tori hadn't talked much about what they'd heard. They barely had time to get Capri groomed and tacked up before Kate's class was called. If only she'd had time to discuss it with her mom or dad, but both were busy keeping everything running smoothly, as well as watching Pete.

"Canter, please. Canter your horses." The announcer's flat voice sounded over the speaker system.

Kate touched Capri with her heel, feeling anew when her

mare instantly picked up the correct lead. She'd only recently learned how to ask properly, and now she understood why Capri had fought her in the past. Getting the proper response from even a well-trained mount depended so much on understanding how to ask. Some of her friends in Spokane thought that riding a horse amounted to climbing into the saddle, kicking the horse, and hauling back on the reins when they wanted to stop.

"Walk your horses, please. Walk your horses."

Kate kept Capri collected as she brought her down to a walk. She'd looked forward to this class for weeks, and now she wasn't even enjoying it. Better to keep her mind on what she was doing for a few minutes, since she couldn't do anything about Melissa or Mocha now—if at all.

They made several more rounds of the arena, reversing direction and putting their horses through their paces yet again. A judge with a clipboard stood in the middle watching each rider as they passed and jotting down notes. Kate wondered if she was writing negative or positive things each time her head bent over the clipboard.

"Form a line in the middle of the arena, please."

The riders did as they were told, then each one backed her horse, then moved forward, taking their original position. Kate hadn't noticed anyone messing up, and she doubted she'd even place with over a dozen riders in this class. It didn't matter anymore. She'd had the fun of taking part, and there was at least one more class she planned to enter later, so there was always hope for a ribbon then.

Each name was called, but Kate barely noticed. Her thoughts had flown ahead to Melissa's dilemma, but as hard as she struggled, she couldn't think of any way to make it better. Did she want to interfere? Melissa wasn't a friend—and at times, Kate felt she was close to an enemy. But something about the girl's reaction to her mother's threat had melted the ice in Kate's heart. She could only imagine what kind of person she'd be if she had a mother like that.

"And second place goes to Kate Ferris riding Capri. Please walk forward and accept your ribbon."

A thrill ran through Kate as she realized they'd called her name. She looked around to be sure—maybe she'd only imagined it—but she saw Tori and Colt on the sidelines clapping and hooting, and her parents grinning not far from her friends. She nudged Capri forward and stroked the mare's neck. "Thank you, big girl. You did it all. I just came along for the ride." New gratitude swelled in her chest that God had brought this horse into her life.

Kate accepted the red ribbon, not caring that it wasn't a first. She'd only been half paying attention during the first several minutes of the class, so it was a wonder she'd placed so high. She rode from the ring, reining to a stop as she reached her parents, Pete, and her friends. She held up the ribbon. "My very first one."

Mom patted Kate's leg. "And I'm sure it won't be your last. You and Tori can be proud of the progress you've made since you started riding. Your dad and I are proud of you too."

"Yeah!" Tori hugged herself. "And I have you guys to thank for it. If it wasn't for Mr. Gray, I wouldn't have gotten a chance to ride in a class at all."

Kate slipped from the saddle and beckoned to the small group. "You guys want to follow me back to my stall?"

Her mom and dad exchanged a look. "Can we stop by in a bit, Kate? We need to get outside and check on the next class that's starting."

"No problem. I'll talk to you later."

Kate listened to Tori and Colt's excited chatter with only half an ear tuned as she considered the startling idea that had popped into her mind. What would her friends think? Or was she crazy?

They paused in front of Capri's stall, and Kate removed her horse's bridle, then slipped a halter over her head. "Anyone got any carrots?"

"No carrots, but I did make a fresh batch of horse treats." Colt whipped a baggie out of his back jeans pocket with a flourish. "I thought you might want some, and since your breeches don't have pockets …" He took a cookie out of the baggie and held it out to the mare. "Yeah, you did a good job, girl," he told Capri. "Only one more class, and you'll get to eat to your heart's content."

Kate drew in a wobbly breath. "Well, that's true, but it might not be exactly what you're thinking about."

Colt's and Tori's heads swiveled her way, and both of them stared.

"Huh?" Tori planted her hands on her hips. "Did you decide to switch classes or something? You aren't going to try a jumping class, I hope. You've only taken one lesson, and Mrs. Jamison said you're not ready."

Kate waved her hand. "I know I'm not. I'd look stupid out there if I tried, and I'd probably end up on my head in the dirt. No, nothing like that."

Colt paused, the baggie of horse treats still in hand, and Capri stretching her neck toward them. "Then what?"

"Well …" She'd better just spit it out. "I was thinking about dropping my class and loaning Capri to Melissa, so she can still compete." The words came out in a rush, and Kate held her breath, wondering what her two friends would say.

Chapter Fifteen

Tori stuck a finger in her ear and jiggled, then pulled it out. "I don't think I heard you right. Did you say you want to loan Capri to Melissa so she can still compete? Are you crazy?"

Colt wagged his head. "It's a nice thought, Kate, but she's never ridden Capri. It would probably be a disaster."

Kate's determination wavered. She'd been so certain her friends would agree. After all, they'd been more friendly and open toward Melissa than she had been over the past few weeks. Now her thoughts drifted to the rest of the show. Getting a second place set her up for possibly earning the silver spurs. If she took two more classes and got a first in both, she might have enough points to win. "Um ..."—she looked from Tori to Colt—"I guess I'm feeling sorry for her. Tori, did you tell Colt what we heard earlier?"

Tori nodded, and her face fell. "I do too, Kate. But it's not right for you to give up your chance to show just because Melissa's horse got injured. That's not your fault."

"But you heard what her mother said. She's going to talk to the vet about giving Mocha some kind of shot for the pain so he can still compete."

"And you heard Melissa say she won't ride him." Tori crossed her arms over her chest. "She's not your responsibility, Kate. She's been rude to you ever since she started boarding here."

Colt sobered. "It's supernice of you, but I don't see how it could work, no matter what."

Kate wanted to laugh. Her friends didn't know her very well if they thought they could talk her out of something she thought was best once she'd made up her mind. In fact, arguing with her was only making her more determined to follow through with her plan. But had she made up her mind completely? *Was* it the right thing to do? Melissa had been rude at times, and even though she was kind to Pete, she'd never acted like she really wanted to be friends with any of them.

Was Tori right that it wasn't her responsibility to fix Melissa's problem? Yeah, Tori had a point. Did Kate really want to give up the chance of winning the silver spurs, even if it wasn't likely to happen? She'd dreamed of this day for a long time—competing and winning ribbons on her own horse. Now she was considering throwing that away, and for what? A girl who didn't deserve it?

Kate studied Colt's and Tori's concerned faces. "I get what you're saying, I really do. And mostly I agree."

"Good. I'm glad that's settled." Tori brushed her hands together. "Now let's groom Capri and get her ready for another class."

Kate shook her head. "Hold it. I'm not done. I said I *mostly* agree. That's not the same thing as totally agreeing."

Colt groaned, but there was a twinkle in his eyes. "Girls. They can be so weird."

Tori elbowed him in the side. "Boys are worse. Now hush, and let Kate talk."

He grinned and held up his hands in surrender. "All right, all right. I know when I'm outnumbered."

Kate fumbled with the girth on Capri's saddle, wondering once again if she was being foolish. "You're cooled off enough now, girl. You can get a little more to eat, and I'll groom you soon." She slipped off the saddle and placed it outside the stall door, then led Capri into the stall and released her. The mare headed straight for the corner feeder.

Kate pivoted and faced her friends, who stood in the open doorway of the stall. She walked outside and slid the door shut behind her. "We need to keep our voices down so no one overhears us. I'm glad Capri's stall is clear down at the end, and the next class doesn't start for an hour."

"Yeah, we're missing the novice hunter-jumper class out-side right now." Tori's usually serene face was creased in a scowl. "Hurry up and say what you're going to say, Kate. Then let's go get something to drink and watch for a bit before you need to groom and tack Capri up again."

Kate's heartbeat calmed. She knew what she was supposed to do now, and nothing was going to stop her.

Tori and Colt reluctantly followed Kate as she went in search of Melissa. Colt sported a cheerful grin as though their mission were perfectly normal, but Tori couldn't seem to completely rid herself of her frown.

Kate understood. She'd probably feel exactly the same if Tori had wanted to loan Mr. Gray to Melissa and give up any chance of competing, but somehow it wasn't the same. Kate had won a red ribbon and was content. This show had never really been about winning the silver spurs; it had been about having fun with her friends and enjoying her horse. Now she had a chance to help some-one else live her dream, and she wasn't going to abandon that.

Colt nudged Tori with his elbow. "Cheer up. I'll bet Melissa will say no anyway. It's not like she's ridden Capri before. She'll see that it's not a good idea and turn Kate down. Then Kate will feel better that she offered, and she can still ride in her next class."

Tori perked up. "Right. So true. Okay, I feel better about this now."

Kate rolled her eyes but didn't reply. She had a feeling it would end differently, but she wasn't going to argue. "Let's check Mocha's stall first. I can't imagine she'd still be there, but you never know."

"She might be guarding Mocha so no one can give her a shot of painkiller." Tori grimaced.

"I'm telling you guys, the vet wouldn't do something like that," Colt insisted. "It's not ethical, even if Melissa's mom insisted."

"Shh." Kate held up her hand. "No using names. No telling who might overhear."

They checked the stall, then moved outside and split up, going from one place to another, hoping to spot Melissa. Finally Kate bumped into her dad. "Where's Pete? I thought he was with you all afternoon."

"Melissa found us. She said she can't ride the rest of the day and asked if she could take Pete to get a snow cone, so I let him go. Nice girl. Pete seems to like her."

"Yeah." Kate winced, but she reminded herself of her decision. She wouldn't let Pete's attachment to Melissa sway her to give up doing the right thing. Jealousy wasn't something she wanted to wallow in, and she pushed it away. "We might need her for some-thing. Can we bring Pete back to you if she ends up being busy?"

"Sure, kiddo. I'll hang out here in the shade and wait for you, just in case."

Kate jogged off across the grass, weaving around children munching hot dogs and parents hollering at little kids not to wander off too far. She could see the concession stand not far ahead and veered that direction. The line was at least ten people deep, with others milling around. Great. She jumped up in the air, hoping to spot Melissa's blonde hair. She wouldn't be wearing her helmet, and there weren't many people in full riding gear in the line, so she should be able to spot her.

Two people left the window holding a snow cone each, and Kate heaved a sigh of relief. Melissa leaned down and tucked a napkin into Pete's hand. Kate quickened her pace as the two turned and headed the opposite direction. "Hey, Melissa, hold up. I need to talk to you." She'd track down Tori and Colt after she explained things to Melissa.

The girl swung around, her hand resting on Pete's head. He didn't pull away or flinch but concentrated on his icy treat. "Kate. Does your dad want me to take Pete back?"

Kate slowed to a stop. "Maybe. I mean, I'm not sure yet." She huffed a breath between her lips. "Sorry for acting weird, but I need to ask you something."

"Whatever." Melissa raised one brow and stared.

Kate gritted her teeth. The girl wasn't making this easy. "I kind of heard a little of what your mom said in the stall."

"You were eavesdropping?" Melissa's stare changed to a glare.

Pete's face scrunched up, and he slapped himself in the forehead two or three times. "Don't get mad. Don't get mad. Don't get mad."

Melissa's face instantly softened, and she knelt beside the little boy. "I'm sorry, buddy. I'm not mad. I'll be nice to Kate, okay?"

"Yes. Be nice. Don't get mad."

"Okay. Will do." She stood and pressed her lips together in a tight line. "Well?"

Kate shivered. She'd allowed the first thing that came to her mind to blurt out instead of thinking this through, and now she'd blown it. "I'm sorry. I was coming to tell you I was sorry about Mocha's injury. I couldn't help but overhear that your mom was upset about it … and that she wanted you to find a way to finish your classes."

"You could have left and not kept listening."

Kate nodded. "I know, but I was afraid you'd hear me leave and think I'd been spying on you. I'm really sorry." At least she'd kept Tori's name out of it.

"Then you also heard me tell her I can't ride, and that's the end of it."

"But you want to, right?"

Melissa's face paled, but her gaze didn't waver. "What do you think?"

"That I asked a stupid question. I'm sorry."

"Quit saying you're sorry and get to the point. Why are you telling me any of this? You could have gone on your way and never let me know, and we'd both be a lot happier." She kept her tone low and her voice controlled, shooting a glance at Pete, who continued to munch on his snow cone.

"Because I think I have a solution."

"What? Shoot my horse up with painkillers like my mother suggested?" Melissa planted her hands on her hips.

Pete looked up and started to rock back and forth. Kate touched his shoulder. "Should we go find Dad, Pete? Want to see what Dad's doing now? I think Rufus is with him. You could hold his leash and lead him around."

"No. Don't get mad. Be nice."

"Okay, will do." She stroked his hair, loving the fact that he didn't pull away. If it wasn't for her little brother, Melissa would probably have stormed off by now and never spoken to her again. Not that it would be a big loss if she did, but Kate was determined to finish this and have her say. "I have an offer to make, if you'll listen."

"Fine. Make it," Melissa said in a deceptively soft voice.

"My horse Capri has a lot of training, but I'm not a good enough rider yet to use her to her full potential—in fact, not even close. She can take up to four-and-a-half-foot jumps. The lady who used to own her rode her in a lot of shows."

Melissa's eyes rounded. "She sounds amazing. But what does that have to do with me?"

"I want to loan her to you so you can compete in the classes you'd need to qualify for regionals."

Melissa stared open-mouthed for several seconds. "Why would you do that? Is this some kind of prank? If I say yes, then you'll snatch it away from me and go off laughing to tell your friends?"

Kate winced. She couldn't believe Melissa would think she'd do something like that. "No way. I'm not that kind of person. I mean it. I want to help."

"But why?" Melissa bit her lip, but not before Kate saw it tremble.

What could she say? That she'd heard the girl sobbing and felt sorry for her? That she thought she had a mean mother and didn't think Melissa should have to suffer at her hands? She doubted Melissa would appreciate either of those reasons. "Because it's the right thing to do."

Melissa regarded her suspiciously. "And you always try to do the right thing, is that it? Are you some kind of do-gooder or what? This isn't making sense. I'm betting you're entered in at least one other class. Why give that up for me?"

Kate fought back her frustration as all the questions started to build. Couldn't the girl say yes and thank you instead of putting her through an inquisition? Sheesh. Right now she wanted to stomp off, find Tori and Colt, and tell them they were right. "Honestly, I'm not even sure why. You haven't been the easiest person to be around since I met you. You've been bossy and demanding and not very friendly. I guess I'm doing it because I'm a Christian. Trust me, if I totally followed my emotions, I'd have walked off and not looked back. But I have to live with myself."

"So you feel sorry for me, is that it? I'm a charity case to you now?"

Kate rolled her eyes. "Get off it, Melissa. Why is it so hard for you to accept a favor that's offered instead of being all high and mighty about it?"

Melissa crossed her arms over her chest and dropped her voice to a near whisper. "Because people don't offer favors unless they expect something in return. What do I have that you want, Kate?"

Kate blinked, not sure she'd heard correctly. "Are you kidding me? Is that what you think? Not a thing. I didn't come here hoping to get something out of you. I figured you might have a chance of winning if you rode Capri, and that's it. Simple. No hidden agenda. If you can't handle it, then I guess that's your problem." She held out her hand to her brother, knowing he'd never take it but wanting to do something. "Pete, let's go find Dad and Rufus."

"Hold it." Melissa's urgent voice halted Kate where she stood. "You're right. I haven't been overly nice to you. I guess recently I've been jealous that you have such a nice mom who wants to be involved in what interests you, and a sweet brother to take care of—not to mention owning a place where you can ride and practice anytime you want to without having to pay." She grimaced. "But I appreciate you offering me your horse, even if I don't get it. I don't think it would work, though. I've never ridden her, and I doubt she'd perform for a stranger."

Hope and excitement surged in Kate. "I've got that all worked out. Your class isn't for another couple of hours, right?"

Melissa nodded.

"There's a practice arena set up in a pasture not far from the show arena. Have you seen it?"

"Sure. Most of the competitors use it to warm up their horses before the jumping classes. I took Mocha over a few jumps there."

"So ride Capri in the warm-up area. Get the feel of her without jumping for the first ten minutes or so, then take her over one low jump. See how she responds, then decide if you want to take it any further. Would you be willing to do that?"

Kate felt someone move up close behind her, and Melissa's gaze strayed past her face and over her shoulder. She pivoted a half turn. Colt and Tori stood behind her, both faces intent and focused on her. She waved a hand. "I told Melissa, and we're discussing how to make this work."

Tori gave a brief nod. "We heard the part about the warm-up arena." She glanced at Melissa. "So you're going to do it?"

Melissa gazed from one face to the other. "I'd like to try, if all of you think it's the right thing to do."

Tori and Colt exchanged a look, then nodded. "We do," Tori said, "and we'll help in any way we can. Let's see if you can win this thing."

Chapter Sixteen

Kate, Tori, and Colt stood near the rail at the outdoor arena, staring in total silence at the jumps inside the fence. Kate gulped and wiped sweaty palms on the jeans she'd changed into when she'd decided to scratch her last class. "They're huge. I mean, gargantuan. Do you think there's any chance Capri can clear those?" Fear rose in her throat and threatened to choke her. Somehow she knew she'd made a mistake allowing Melissa to ride her horse.

Colt turned a calm gaze her way. "I forgot to ask. Does your mom know you're letting Melissa use Capri?"

"Yeah. I asked her, and she said it was okay." She ducked her head for a moment. "She said she was proud of me that I'd want to offer."

"Great. So these poles are set at three-foot and three-foot-six inches. She didn't have any trouble in the warm-up arena on jumps six inches to a foot lower. In fact, she cleared them with that much or more to spare."

Tori gripped her hands so tight on the top rail that her knuckles turned white. "I sure hope you're right, Colt. They look big to me too." She moved closer to Kate. "I'm sorry. That was a dumb thing to say. I should be trying to make you feel better, not worrying out loud."

"You're being honest, and that's okay. But yeah, I am worried, and I'm glad Colt thinks she can make them." In spite of the warm day, she shivered. "Melissa is a good rider. I guess partly I'm afraid Capri might get hurt the same way Mocha did."

Tori kept her eyes glued to the riders walking the course. "But look at all the horses who've jumped today, and not one of them has been injured. I think that was a freak accident."

Kate smiled at her friend's obvious attempt to cheer her. "Thanks, Tori. I hope that's true."

Colt swished the ever-present blade of grass to the side of his mouth. "Are you wishing you hadn't let her use Capri? It's not too late to call it off. She's the third person to compete, so there's time to scratch. It's your call, you know. I'm sure Melissa would understand. It's not like she came to you asking to use your horse."

Kate couldn't believe how tempting that suggestion was—and even more, how long it took her to think about it before she made a decision. What a relief it would be to have Capri pulled from the competition and know she was safe. "No, that wouldn't be fair. I've never seen Melissa so excited and ... happy."

It was true. She'd truly never seen Melissa with so much joy on her face as when she'd taken Capri over the practice jumps, and again later, as she exited the ring and thanked Kate for the tenth time. Kate couldn't get over it. Would the girl revert to her old self once the show was over and she had no more need of Kate or her horse?

Colt lifted an arm and pointed. "Look. The riders are finished walking the course, and they're getting ready to send in the first rider."

Kate wrapped her arms around herself, trying to stop shivering. She was as excited as she was scared. It was pretty awesome owning a horse who could compete at this level. If only she were the one getting to ride her instead of Melissa. But that wasn't fair— she didn't have a clue how to put a horse over those kinds of jumps, much less stay on, and it wasn't like she'd ever hoped to compete at jumping anytime soon. Maybe someday. At least she could dream.

A big black-bay Thoroughbred gelding entered the ring, with a girl who looked to be about sixteen riding him. She cantered around the perimeter one time, then headed for the first jump. The clock mounted on a pole at the end of the arena started flashing through the seconds as soon as she crossed in front of the starter.

Tori leaned over to Kate. "So this class has penalties for jumps knocked down as well as penalties if they go over the time allowed, right?"

"Yes. The horses shouldn't have to rush too fast, but if they hesitate between jumps or swing too wide very often, they could go over the time limit and pick up faults."

They watched in silence as the gelding took the first four jumps with ease, seeming to not even notice they were there. As he neared the fifth, he stumbled and broke stride. His rider tightened her reins and corrected quickly, but the horse couldn't regain his speed in time to clear the jump. His forelegs rapped against the pole, and it clattered to the ground. A groan swept through the crowd lining the rails. He launched himself over the final series of three jumps, but he seemed to lose heart. He barely cleared the first two, then his hind hooves dragged the rail from the standard on the third, and it clattered to the ground. The rider patted the horse's neck as she pointed him toward the exit.

The announcer's voice echoed from the speakers. "Eight jumping faults for Susan Meyers, riding Felix's Dynamo."

"Too bad for them," Colt said. "But good for us."

A bubble of hope formed, but Kate refused to allow it to grow. There were eight entries in this class, and it had been almost two years since Capri had been put through her paces in a jumping arena.

Tori nudged Kate's elbow. "Here comes the next one. Wow! He's big."

Colt nodded. "Looks like a stallion. I'll bet that boy is powerful."

Kate's heart sank. "Yeah, he'll probably clear every jump without any problem at all."

The big chestnut approached the first jump and cleared it with at least six inches to spare, then cantered on to the next, taking it with no hesitation and plenty of room.

Colt pointed to the clock. "Look. He's doing great on the course, but he's taking all his corners wide, and his rider isn't asking for any speed. He's slower than the first horse."

Kate hadn't noticed, but now that Colt pointed it out, she realized that even with his long stride, the stallion barely seemed to be cantering. "What's wrong with his rider? You'd think she'd push him harder."

"Maybe she isn't watching the clock, but she should be," Colt said. "It's going to be close."

The chestnut took the final two jumps, clearing them with ease, then moved in a rocking-horse canter toward the line where the clock had started. The announcer's voice boomed again. "No jumping faults for Razmataz, ridden by Carly Simpson." There was a smattering of applause. "However, he earned three time faults."

Kate reached out and grabbed Tori's hand. "Here they come."

Melissa entered the ring, sitting confidently as the chestnut mare cantered easily around the perimeter of the ring. She headed for the start line, and Kate held her breath. "Please, God. Please, God. Let her do well." She didn't realize she'd spoken out loud until she felt Tori squeeze her hand.

Melissa sat forward in three-point position, her gaze trained on the first jump and her hands steady on the reins. Capri gathered her legs under herself and seemed to float over the rail. She landed on the turf, and Melissa turned the mare's head toward the next obstacle, a vertical double rail. Melissa asked for a little more speed, then checked the mare as she neared the jump, and she sailed over it with inches to spare. She took the next one without hesitation as well.

Tori gasped. "She makes that look so easy! But why does she speed her up and then slow her down? That doesn't make sense."

Kate kept her gaze on Capri and Melissa as she answered. "Mrs. Jamison told me it's up to the rider to gauge the number of strides the horse will need to take between jumps, and how fast or slow to ask it to go. That's one of the reasons they walk the course ahead of time. Melissa probably thought it was the right speed to make that jump, then realized she needed to slow Capri down to clear it."

Capri rounded the last corner and headed for the triple, each set with only two long strides between. Was her horse in good enough condition to hold up and make a clear run? Kate glanced at the clock. It was going to be close to not earn time faults.

Tori's hand tightened on her own as Capri launched herself over the first obstacle, then took two long strides between and cleared the second. "One more, only one more." Kate chanted the words, praying she'd make it.

Melissa leaned far over the horse's neck, seeming to will her to make the final attempt. Capri sailed into the air, but as her back hooves rose over the rail, they clanged against the wood.

Kate winced and watched the rail wobble in place. "Please don't fall, please don't fall, please don't fall." The rail stayed in place, and a cheer rose from the crowd.

Capri cantered toward the finish line and crossed it with a half second to spare on the clock.

"A clear round for Melissa Tolbert, riding Capri, owned by Kate Ferris."

Tori squealed and thumped Kate on the back. "They said your name too! Cool! That's almost as good as being able to ride her yourself. She did it, Kate. She didn't get any faults!"

Kate grinned, allowing herself a few seconds to rejoice, then sobered. "Yeah. I'm excited too, but she hasn't won yet. There are still five more horses to go."

"Wow. Oh, wow." Kate stared from one of her friends to the other. "I can't believe that last horse refused the jump twice and got disqualified."

Colt nodded. "And the one before that knocked down a rail. Of all eight of the entries, three of them rode a clear round."

Tori jumped up and down. "What happens next? Does that mean they flip a coin on who gets first, second, and third, or what?"

Kate giggled. "No, they have a jump-off."

Tori crinkled her nose. "What's that mean?"

"They remove a couple of the jumps to make the course shorter, and all three horses with clear rounds will do it over again. And this time, they'll time each rider. If none of them knock down any rails, then the one who makes the best time wins."

"So Capri has to do it again? Do you think she's too tired?"

"I hope not. At least she was one of the first to go, so she's had time to recover. Come on, let's go find Melissa and see what she thinks."

It only took two minutes to find Melissa standing beside Capri, holding her reins and stroking her neck. Kate pushed aside her flicker of jealousy. She should be thankful this girl was kind to her horse—in fact, she would never have allowed Melissa to ride Capri if she wasn't.

"Hey, Melissa!" Kate lifted her hand. "You guys did great! We're rooting for you to win the jump-off." She rubbed Capri's forehead beneath her forelock, wishing she'd thought to bring a carrot. "How is Capri holding up? Do you think she can handle another round?"

Melissa's eyes sparkled. "Yes, I do. She's an amazing horse— very strong and confident. It's like she hasn't been away from competition at all. It's a short course and with two jumps removed, so it's not as demanding." She directed a meaningful look at Kate. "You're very lucky to have her."

"I know. I wouldn't have her if God hadn't answered my prayer and given her to me."

Melissa arched her brows but didn't respond. She stepped to Capri's side and checked her girth. "I guess it's time to cinch you up, girl, and head back to the ring."

Tori edged forward. "Are you going to walk the course again?"

"No. We only get to do that on the first round. It's basically the same course. They're just removing a couple of the jumps. I've been going over it in my mind, working out Capri's speed and strides. I hope I don't mess up."

It was the first time Kate had seen Melissa less than confident. "Hey, we'll all pray you do your best. That's all that matters, right?"

Melissa snorted. "Not to my mom, but I'll take whatever help I can get." She gave Kate a tiny smile that still hinted of nerves. "Thanks."

A few minutes later, the announcer called the start of the class. Kate grabbed Tori's hand and beckoned to Colt. "We'd better hurry. Good luck, Melissa and Capri!"

They bounded across the grass to the far side of the arena, closest to the final three jumps. The loudspeaker crackled. "Up first is Tom Jenkins, riding Carrousel."

The gray Thoroughbred circled the ring before charging toward the first jump. It was obvious his rider was determined to finish in the lowest amount of time. He cleared the first two jumps and galloped toward the final set of three.

The rider hauled back on his reins, attempting to check the big gelding's rush, but the speed appeared to have gone to his head. He bolted over the first jump without touching the bar, but his speed had lengthened his stride to the point that he took the second one too late, his front legs slamming into the bar.

A collective groan went up from the crowd, but Colt gave a tiny victory jab with his fist and leaned toward Kate and Tori. "Not that I'm wishing anyone bad luck, but that sure gives Melissa and Capri a better chance."

"Four faults for Carrousel, ridden by Tom Jenkins. No time faults. Entering the ring next is Carol Saunders, riding Majesty's Wonder."

A smattering of applause met the snow-white mare that cantered into the ring, the rider looking in perfect control of her mount. After taking the mandatory loop, the mare headed for the first jump. She nailed it dead center with plenty of room to spare, then cleared the second in the same fashion.

Kate couldn't remove her eyes from the gorgeous mare. "Wow. She's awesome. And that girl really knows how to ride."

She watched as the horse took the corner at a fast pace and galloped toward the final set of three, her rhythm and speed looking flawless. She soared over the first and second jump, then hesitated slightly before clearing the third with a slight rub that didn't knock down the rail. She crossed the line, and the clock stopped several seconds ahead of the first rider, to the sound of cheers from the crowd.

Kate's hopes plummeted. She didn't see any possible way Capri could compete against that.

"Carol Saunders, riding Majesty's Wonder, completed a clean round with zero time faults. Our final rider is Melissa Tolbert, riding Capri, owned by Kate Ferris."

Kate tried to hide her grin but couldn't quite manage it. She was so proud of her horse. Even if she got third, she didn't care—that was more than she'd hoped for or would have been able to win if she'd been riding. But for Melissa's sake, she prayed she'd do better.

Capri and Melissa entered and cantered around the edge of the arena. Just before Capri crossed the line to start the clock, the mare stumbled, and a soft gasp rose from the spectators. Melissa picked up the mare's head with her reins and urged Capri forward, briefly stroking her neck, then tightened her reins.

"Come on, girl, you can do this." Kate whispered the words, almost afraid to speak.

A hint of moisture showed on Capri's neck, but the mare didn't seem to be laboring as she headed toward the first jump and took it with ease. The spectators seemed to release a collective sigh, and Kate's hope increased a notch. Only four more to go.

Capri barreled down on the second jump at a higher rate of speed than Kate had seen thus far. She sailed over it with inches to spare, then cut the corner at a fast clip and galloped on to the set of three.

Colt gripped her shoulder on one side, and Tori squeezed her hand on the other. Kate's parents and Pete stood across the arena. She'd noticed them seconds before Capri entered the ring, but she was grateful for the presence of her friends. She didn't think she could have stood the stress on her own, even though she knew her parents would have been there for her if she'd asked.

Capri launched herself over the first jump, landed, and took one long bound before clearing the second. Her feet hit the turf between the two jumps. She took two shorter strides and bounded over the final hurdle without so much as a rub. Melissa rode like a jockey now, up on the mare's neck, urging her around the final turn and into the homestretch. She crossed the line as cheers erupted around the arena, with the loudest shouts coming from Kate and her friends.

Kate wanted to climb through the rails, run to her horse, and throw her arms around her. She had no idea what her time had been and couldn't remember what time she had to beat, but she was proud of Melissa and Capri, regardless. She spun on Colt. "The time? How did she do on the time?"

"Don't know," he admitted. "I was so excited, I didn't pay attention to what the other rider got. But she rode totally clean!"

Tori thumped Kate on the back while screaming in her ear, "She did it, Kate. I just know it."

The crowd quieted as the speaker system crackled again. "Melissa Tolbert, riding Capri, also completed a clear round with no faults. We'd like all three riders to bring their horses to the center of the ring, please, to get your ribbons."

Carrousel, Majesty's Wonder, and Capri lined up where instructed, their riders still in their saddles. A hush blanketed the crowd as the shuffling of papers sounded clearly over the speaker. What was taking so long?

The announcer cleared his throat. "Third place goes to Carrousel, owned and ridden by Tom Jenkins, with four jumping

faults and no time faults. Congratulations on a job well done."
The crowd applauded as a young girl stepped forward to present
a huge white ribbon with a rosette in the center.

"Second place and first place were less than one second
apart, so the judges had to make a decision, as this would tech-
nically be considered a tie at this age level. Due to the fact that
Majesty's Wonder rubbed the final rail and Capri did not have
any rubs, second place goes to Majesty's Wonder, owned and
ridden by Carol Saunders. Congratulations on a great ride."

Kate shrieked, not at the second-place win, but at what
that meant for Melissa and Capri. "I can't believe it. I can-
not believe it!" She grabbed Tori and hugged her so tight,
her friend gave a little squeal. "Sorry." She released her and
stepped away.

"And finally, first place, as well as the high-point winner for
this show, earning a set of silver spurs, is Melissa Tolbert, riding
Capri, owned by Kate Ferris. If Kate Ferris is in the crowd, could
you please come join Miss Tolbert and Capri?"

Kate's heart jolted, and her feet froze in place.

Colt hissed at her and gave her a shove. "So get moving. You
are Kate Ferris, right?" His happy grin woke her up, and Kate
crawled through the bars, praying she wouldn't faint.

She jogged across the seemingly endless expanse of grass,
then came to a stop beside Capri's shoulder. Joy like nothing

she'd ever known filled her, and she whispered under her breath, "Thank You, God, so much." She stroked Capri's shoulder, not caring that it was sweaty. Right now she could lay her face on it and cry, she was so happy.

The young girl presenting the ribbons came forward and handed Melissa the blue rosette and an open box containing a pair of burnished silver spurs. Melissa stood still while a photographer snapped a picture of the three of them, then she leaned toward Kate, extending the ribbon. "This is Capri's. She earned it, not me. You're one lucky girl, Kate, and I'm honored I got a chance to ride her."

Kate accepted the ribbon with trembling fingers, hoping she wouldn't drop it. This was more than she'd ever expected. Nothing in the world could ever top this.

Epilogue

Kate, Tori, and Colt lounged on the grass next to the fence surrounding the outdoor arena. Kate snickered and pointed at Tori's hair. "You're no longer a dark brunette. You have white highlights."

Tori made a face. "Well, you have white freckles all over your face and hands, so I guess we're even."

Kate narrowed her eyes at Colt. "How come you don't have any paint anywhere, huh? It sure looks like you've been loafing while the two of us have been working."

Colt leaned back on his hands and smirked. "Nope. I happen to be a professional, while you girls are amateurs, that's all. Leave it to a guy to do a job right."

Kate picked up her brush and flipped it at Colt. It didn't have much paint on it, but a few dozen tiny drops flecked his face, hair, and neck. She giggled and grabbed his brush before he could. "Professional, huh? Well, this *girl* is faster than you are, so there."

He gave a pretend glower, then laughed. "Guess you won that one. Hey, have you guys seen Melissa since the show? It's been three days, and she hasn't been around that I've seen."

Kate made a face. "As far as I know, she hasn't been here at all except once when I was gone. I've been wondering if she's going to move her horse somewhere else, or maybe she's sick or something."

Tori smoothed her palm over the grass beside her. "Seems kind of weird after you let her ride Capri and all. I know she thanked you at the show, but I thought she'd at least come around afterward. I didn't even get a chance to see her spurs."

Kate nodded. "Yeah, I know. I've been wondering if she's going back to how she was before. You know, she made her mom happy, got what she wanted by winning the points she needed to move on to the next level, and now she'll be a snottier Melissa than ever."

"Anything's possible, I guess," Colt said.

Kate handed him his brush and picked up her own. "We'd better get this fence finished. I promised Dad we'd do it today. He and Mom want to get this place dressed up and make some improvements. We made enough from the show to buy stall mats for all the boarders' stalls."

"Cool." Tori dipped her brush in the paint can and swiped it across a rail. "Hey, who's that?" She pointed at a car driving into the parking area.

Kate shaded her eyes against the sun. "I'm not sure."

They waited until the door opened and a figure stepped out of the passenger seat—one dressed in old jeans and a scruffy T-shirt. "Melissa," Kate breathed. "She must have come to change Mocha's leg wrap. Mom said she came one other day, but I missed her."

The girl didn't head toward the barn but strode toward them, hands in her back pockets. She glanced from one face to the other and smiled, then started to giggle. Kate stiffened. This was exactly what she'd expected. The high-and-mighty Melissa Tolbert intended to make fun of how they looked. "What's the problem?"

Melissa sobered and pulled a paintbrush from her back pocket. "I brought my own. If I help, will you promise not to turn me into a towhead, like Tori?" Her eyes sparkled as she glanced at Tori, then back to Kate.

"Huh?" Kate shook her head, not certain she'd heard correctly. "How did you know we were painting? I'm sure you don't carry a paintbrush with you wherever you go."

Melissa grinned. "I called and talked to your mom. I asked what you guys were doing. I was going to see if you wanted to go have a Coke or something, but she said you were all painting the fence. So I decided you'd get finished faster if I helped. But not unless you promise not to make me look like him." She pointed at Colt this time and giggled again.

Kate couldn't believe her ears. "Seriously? You want to help *us*?"

Melissa's smile faded. "If you'll have me."

Colt grinned. "Fine by me. But you have to fit in, or no can do." He flipped his brush at her and smirked. "Now you look like the rest of us, and we'd be happy to have your help."

She rolled her eyes and dipped her brush in the paint can, then held it up threateningly. "I have a pretty good aim, so I'd be careful if I were you." She shook it at him and laughed, then turned toward Kate. "I owe you big-time," she said in a serious tone. "My mom was ashamed when she found out you'd overheard us and sacrificed your classes for me. When I told her you guys were painting and said it was the least I could do to say thanks, she drove me here. I hope you'll forgive me for the way I've treated you guys. I'd like to be friends, if that's possible."

A sense of peace washed over Kate. She tugged on Melissa's free hand. "Sit. We're lazy painters, but we can use all the help we can get." She flashed a smile. "Besides, you can never have too many friends."

When a rockin' concert comes to an end,
the audience might cheer for an encore.
When a tasty meal comes to an end,
it's always nice to savor a bit of dessert.
When a great story comes to an end,
we think you may want to linger.
And so we offer ...

... just a little something more after
you have finished a David C Cook novel.
We invite you to stay awhile in the story.
Thanks for reading!

Turn the page for ...

Secrets for Your Diary

Secret #1

Kate, Tori, and Colt all share a love of horses. But they share something else too. All three have been treated as if they don't exist by the "popular crowd." Kate's the new kid at school, Tori is from a low-income home and doesn't look like everyone else, and Colt is homeschooled.

Have you ever felt ignored at school or at any other activity? How did you handle that feeling? Did being ignored make you think of yourself differently? How did you respond to those in the in-crowd as a result? Who helped you during this tough time? What did that person say or do that made a difference?

Note from Kate

Sometimes we feel all alone—like no one else has ever experienced what we're going through. Believe it or not, your parents and teachers were your age once and probably went through something similar. And the Bible says that Jesus experienced rejection and pain too. Don't ever be afraid to talk to Him or to an adult you trust about hard things you're dealing with. There are people who care and want to help.

Secret #2

Kate feels a flicker of jealousy when Colt and Tori think Melissa does a good job jumping Mocha. Tori notices Kate's reaction. A short time later, when Tori and Kate discuss Melissa, they have no idea she's listening. They're joking, but Melissa doesn't take it that way. She flings back, "I can't imagine being friends with either of you, or why you'd think I'd care to be."

Have you ever overheard someone talking about you? How did that make you feel? Or have you been caught talking about someone else? What did the person you were talking about say or do? Why do you think Melissa said what she did? What would you have said or done if you had been Melissa?

Note from Kate

Many times people say things because they're hurting and don't want anyone to know. Before you get angry, take a minute and put yourself in their place. They might have had a horrible day or come from a bad home life that makes them want to hurt others. Praying for them can make a huge difference in how you feel about them, and it might even help them change too!

Secret #3

Melissa's actions, in general, drove Kate crazy. After all, who would want to hang out with a girl who is as snotty as Melissa? But then Kate is surprised by Melissa's gentle treatment of Pete, feels bad that Melissa took a bad fall and got spooked, and overhears the pressured conversation between Melissa and her mother. Those three events begin to change Kate's view of Melissa and why she acts the way she does.

When has a person you don't like very much surprised you by doing something kind? Tell the story. How did that event change your view of that person? When bad things happen to people you don't like, how do you respond? Do you feel bad, like Kate did? Or do you say to yourself, *Well, she/he deserved it*? How might you respond instead so that you, like Kate, can make a friend?

Note from Kate

Try an experiment. Find someone who's not kind to you and do something nice for that person. Don't do it hoping he or she will change but because it's the right thing to do, and you never know if your actions might make a difference in that person's life. I know it's not easy to be kind to someone who's mean, but if nothing else, pray for him or her and ask God to work a miracle—in your life or the other person's.

Colt's Favorite Horse Cookies

Colt enjoyed baking treats for his horse. You can too. Here is his favorite, easy recipe.

What you'll need:
   *2 cups flour
   *2 cups oatmeal (uncooked, regular oatmeal, not "quick oatmeal")
   *2 cups shredded carrots
   *2 tablespoons white sugar
   *2 teaspoons salt
   *1/2 cup water
   *4 tablespoons corn oil
   *1/2 cup molasses
   *2 mixing bowls
   *Pam (or some other liquid baking spray)
   *2 cookie sheets

Extra, if desired:
   *1 apple, finely diced into pieces (but cookies fall apart more easily with the apple in it)

1. Preheat oven to 350 degrees and spray cookie sheets with Pam.

2. In a bowl, mix the flour, oatmeal, carrots, sugar, and salt.

3. In the second bowl, mix the water, oil, and molasses.

4. Pour the wet mixture into the dry mixture and stir well with a spoon (or your fingers for fun!).

5. Form mixture into small balls and place one inch apart on cookie sheets.

6. Bake at 350 degrees for 15 minutes or until golden brown.

These horse treats also freeze well.

Author's Note

I've been an avid horse lover all of my life. I can't remember a time when I wasn't fascinated with the idea of owning a horse, although it didn't happen until after I married. As I was growing up, my family lived in a small town on a couple of acres that were mostly steep hillside, so other than our lawn and garden area, there was no room for a horse. I lived out my dreams by reading every book I could find that had anything to do with horses.

My first horse was a two-year-old Arabian gelding named Nicky, who taught me so much and caused me to fall deeply in love with the Arabian breed. Over the years we've owned a stallion, a number of mares, a handful of foals, and a couple of geldings. It didn't take too many years to discover I couldn't make money in breeding. After losing a mare and baby due to a reaction to penicillin, and having another mare reject her baby at birth, we decided it was time to leave that part of the horse industry and simply enjoy owning a riding horse or two.

Our daughter, Marnee, brought loving horses to a whole new level. She was begging to ride when she was two to three years old and was riding her own pony alone at age five. Within a few years, she requested lessons, as she wanted to switch from Western trail riding to showing English, both in flat work and hunt-seat, and later, in basic dressage. I learned so much listening to her instructor and watching that I decided to take lessons myself.

We spent a couple of years in the show world, but Marnee soon discovered she wanted to learn for the sake of improving her own skills more than competing, and she became a first-rate horsewoman.

We still ride together, as she and her husband, Brian, own property next to ours. My old Arabian mare, Khaila, was my faithful trail horse for over seventeen years and lived with Marnee's horses on their property, so she wouldn't be lonely. At the age of twenty-six, she began having serious age-related problems and went on to horse heaven in late July of 2013. I ride Brian's Arabian mare, Sagar, now when Marnee and I trail-ride. I am so blessed to have a daughter who shares the same love as I do and to have had so many wonderful years exploring the countryside with my faithful horse Khaila.

If you don't own your own horse yet, don't despair. It might not happen while you still live at home, and you might have to live out your dreams in books, or even by taking a lesson at a local barn, but that's okay. God knows your desire and will help fulfill it in His perfect way.

Acknowledgments

This series has been a brand-new adventure for me—one I never expected, but one I'm so blessed to have experienced. I've loved horses all my life and owned them since I was nineteen, but I never thought I'd write horse novels for girls. I'm so glad I was wrong!

So many people have helped make this series possible: My friends at church, who were excited when I shared God's prompting and offered to pray that the project would find a home, as well as my family, my agent, and my critique group, who believed in me, listened, read my work, and cheered me on. There have also been a number of authors who helped me brainstorm ideas for the series or specific sections of one book or the other when I struggled—Kimberly, Vickie, Margaret, Cheryl, Lissa, Nancy—you've all been such a blessing!

But there's a special group of kids I especially want to thank. A huge thank-you to Caitlyn Baker who was the first one to read the early chapter of this book, before I had a contract. Every Sunday after church she'd track me down and beg for more—and ask when it was going to be published. That little girl spurred me on to keep writing, and I owe her a huge thank-you for her confidence and support. Also, two different times I posted on Facebook, asking my readers if they had a child who might be willing to read a couple of chapters and give me honest feedback. A number of people responded, and I had my test group of kids. I want to thank Elly, Bella, Payzlie, Cadence, Alexis, Kyra, Hannah, Kasie, Kylie, Crystal, Amber, Haley, Annika, Katelyn, Karli, Jessi, Hailee, Camille, Kayla, and Elena.

Thanks also to Kayla L. Tucker, a fifteen-year-old horse enthusiast who created Colt's Favorite Horse Cookies recipe and happily allowed me to use it in this book.

I also want to thank the team at David C Cook. I was so thrilled when Don Pape asked if I'd consider sending this series to him to review when I mentioned I was writing it. The horse lovers on the committee snatched it up and galloped with it, and I was so excited! I love working with this company and pray we'll have many more years and books together. Thank you to all who made this a possibility and, we pray, a resounding success!

Thank you for taking the time to read my new series, and watch for another book in three months!

About the Author

Miralee Ferrell, the author of the Horses and Friends series plus twelve other novels, was always an avid reader. She started collecting first-edition Zane Grey Westerns as a young teen. But she never felt the desire to write books … until after she turned fifty. Inspired by Zane Grey and old Western movies, she decided to write stories set in the Old West in the 1880s.

After she wrote her first western novel, *Love Finds You in Last Chance, California*, she was hooked. Her *Love Finds You in Sundance, Wyoming* won the Will Rogers Medallion Award for Western fiction, and Universal Studios requested a copy of her debut novel, *The Other Daughter*, for a potential family movie.

Miralee loves horseback riding on the wooded trails near her home with her married daughter, who lives nearby, and spending time with her granddaughter, Kate. Besides her horse friends, she's owned cats, dogs (a six-pound, long-haired Chihuahua named Lacey was often curled up on her lap as she wrote this book), rabbits, chickens, and even two cougars,

Spunky and Sierra, rescued from breeders who couldn't care for them properly.

Miralee would love to hear from you:

www.miraleeferrell.com (blog and website)
www.twitter.com/miraleeferrell
www.facebook.com/miraleeferrell
www.facebook.com/groups/82316202888 (fan group)

Sneak Peek at Book Three: Mystery Rider

Chapter One

Upper Hood River Valley, Odell, Oregon
Summer, Present Day

Kate Ferris sprawled on the grass next to the newly painted paddock fence on her parents' farm. "Thanks for your help, guys. It sure goes faster with more than one person working." She shot a sideways glance at Melissa Tolbert, still barely able to believe the girl who had always been so snotty at school had shown up and offered to help. "You're not bad at slapping on paint."

Melissa leaned back on her elbows and grinned. "Even if Colt didn't keep his word to not splatter me with it."

Freckle-faced Colt Turner removed a long piece of straw from between his lips. "Hey, you said not to make you look like the rest of us, but I didn't make any promises."

Tori Velasquez, Kate's best friend, rolled her eyes. "We should get the brushes cleaned and the rest of the paint closed up and put away before you two start fighting again."

"Not fighting." Melissa arched one blonde brow. "Just discussing."

"Whatever." Tori smiled. "I was kinda wondering ..." She eyed Melissa.

"Yeah?"

"Well, I never got to see those spurs you won while showing Capri. I don't suppose you've got them in your back pocket or anything."

Kate snorted a laugh. "Now that would be funny—no, not funny, painful. Melissa wouldn't dare sit if she did. Could you bring them over sometime so we can all see them?" Pivoting toward Melissa, Kate was surprised at the girl's suddenly serious expression. "Of course, you don't have to. It's not a big deal." The last thing Kate wanted was for the recent truce between Melissa, herself, and her two best friends to be ruined.

Melissa turned away for a minute, then back. "I'll do better than that. They really should be yours—or at least belong to the barn, since it was your horse I rode, Kate. How about I bring them over and give them to you?" she asked, her face earnest.

Kate shook her head, her long brown braids swinging. "No way! Mom and Dad would never agree, and I don't either. You won those spurs fair and square. You gave me the blue ribbon to put on Capri's stall door, and that's good enough. If you hadn't been such a good rider, Capri wouldn't have won the championship. There's no way I'd have made her jump that well."

Spots of pink appeared on Melissa's cheeks, and she ducked her head. "Okay. Thanks." She raised her eyes and stared at each of them in turn. "So, are you guys entering the Fort Dalles parade this summer?"

"Huh?" Kate lifted one brow. "I only moved here in March. I'm not sure I know what or where that is."

Tori poked Kate in the side with her elbow. "Up the river at The Dalles, silly. The rodeo and parade are for Fort Dalles Days, 'cause that's what it was at first—a fort, way over a hundred years ago. It's pretty cool. They have a carnival, rodeo, parade, and other stuff, and it lasts a week or so." She turned to Melissa. "But why would any of us want to enter the parade?"

Colt sat up straight, and his blue eyes brightened. "The barn. Right, Melissa? You're thinking Kate and her parents should do something in the parade to advertise the boarding stable here?"

Melissa shrugged. "Yeah, why not?"

Kate wrapped one of her braids around her finger. "It's way too hard and expensive to build a float."

Melissa nodded. "Right. But how about riding your horses and making banners to put over their hindquarters, behind their saddles? You could even dress them or yourselves up if you wanted to. Cowgirls"—she shot Colt a look—"or cowboys ... or just wear your English riding gear, and Colt can be the cowboy. It doesn't matter so much what you wear, but I think it's a good idea to be in the parade. It's a cheap way to let people know you're open for business."

"I like it!" Kate gazed at each of her friends. "So, are you guys in? Do you want to ride your horses in the parade and help us advertise the barn?"

Tori's dark-brown eyes widened, and she pulled back. "I don't know, Kate. What if my horse gets scared at all the noise, and I can't handle him? It's not like I'm an expert rider like Melissa, or even as good as you or Colt."

Melissa waved her fingers. "Hey, I wasn't trying to push in. I only suggested it for you guys. You don't need to include me."

Kate tipped her head. "You aren't getting out of it that easy, Melissa Tolbert. This was your idea, so you're stuck with us, since you seem to know so much about what we're supposed to do."

A shrill tone sounded in Melissa's pocket, and she took out a cell phone. "Sorry, guys. My mom. I'll be right back." She pushed to her feet and walked a few yards away, keeping her back to the group. Her voice dropped, but a light breeze pushed her words toward Kate and her friends. "Yeah. Just hanging out with those kids from the barn. No big deal. I can leave if you don't want me here."

Colt leaned forward and whispered to Kate and Tori, "Her mom was pretty pushy about her earning the most points at the horse show. I wonder if she'll want Melissa helping us. We're not exactly rich or anything. She might not want to hang around." He contorted his face into one of his trademark comical expressions.

Kate laughed. "I wondered that too." She sobered. "And to be honest, whether this *new* Melissa will last. From what she said to her mom, it doesn't sound like being here is a big deal to her. I want to trust her, but after the way she treated us at school and then bossed us around when she came to the barn, I'm not sure I can."

"I think we need to be nice to her," dark-haired Tori replied. "She didn't have to help with the fence or give us suggestions for the parade. How about inviting her to our sleepover tonight? We could start planning what we want to do for the parade."

"I think that's pushing things too fast," Kate said. "I agree with Colt. We're not in Melissa's circle of friends, and I doubt she'd even want to come. How about we ask if she wants to be part of our parade group and nothing more for now?"

Someone's throat cleared behind the group, and they all turned. Melissa stood, frowning, several feet away. "Are you talking about me?"

"Sorry, Melissa. We were talking about the parade and wondering if you'd want to help." Tori paused. "We were thinking Colt could be in charge, since he's the only guy."

Colt raised his hands and laughed. "No way. I'm no organizer, but I'm guessing Melissa would be good at that kind of thing. I vote for Melissa."

Tori clapped. "I second it!"

Kate nodded. "It's decided. Melissa's the head of our parade committee, if she agrees." She exchanged glances with Tori. She knew what her kindhearted friend was thinking. They needed to invite Melissa to come tonight. It was the right thing to do. But Kate bet they'd end up being sorry.

"Seriously? You guys want me to help?" Melissa, seemingly rooted to the ground, gazed around the small semicircle.

"Yep." Kate smiled. "But don't take it as too big a of compliment. You might end up being sorry you ever agreed. If you'll do it, and our parents agree, then you're it."

The uncertainty in Melissa's green eyes turned to acceptance, and a hint of joy seemed to shine through. "Right. So when do you want to start planning?"

Kate and Tori looked at each other. Colt was coming to the party for popcorn and a movie, then planned to go home while the two girls stayed up in Kate's room talking and giggling. Did Kate really want to include Melissa in their private party when she'd been such a pain in the past, dissing them and being so condescending? Tori gave a tiny nod. Kate sneaked a glance at Colt, who barely shrugged one shoulder.

Melissa searched Kate's face. "What's up? Am I missing something?"

"Nope. You're not going to miss a thing. In fact, if you're free tonight, we'll start planning after we eat a big bowl of popcorn. You wanna come to my house tonight?"

Melissa stared at Kate as if stunned. "With all of you?"

"Yeah. Me, Tori, and Colt. We were going to have a sleepover, but I don't know if you'd want to do that."

Colt nearly choked on his straw and blew it out of his mouth. "Hey, now. You're going to ruin my reputation. I am *not* staying for the sleepover. Just the food and a movie—unless we change it to food and talking about the parade. Got it?"

Kate giggled. "Like my parents would allow a guy to stay the night, or like we'd want you to." She wrinkled her nose. "No offense, Colt, but your socks stink when you take your shoes off, and no matter how nice you are, we don't want any guys crashing our girl time."

"Good!" Colt heaved a huge sigh. "You had me scared for a minute there. But I'm in for popcorn and planning, if everyone else wants to do that."

Melissa nodded slowly. "Okay. I know my mom won't care. I'll come for the popcorn and to talk about the parade, but I don't think I can stay long—not for the sleepover anyway. I've got something else I need to do tonight … and honestly, I'm not sure you guys would want me around that long."

Kate jumped in. "We didn't say that, Melissa. I just wasn't sure you'd feel comfortable hanging out with us for a longer time—you know, after all that's happened in the past. But you can if you'd like. Really."

"Thanks …" Melissa hesitated. "But not this time. I really am busy later tonight."

A small smile flickered across her lips, as if she had a secret she wasn't telling. Kate winced inwardly. She'd seen that same expression before when Melissa was scheming something that wouldn't be fun for the rest of them. She and Tori had been on the receiving end of the wealthy girl's meanness too many times. As for Colt, he seemed to ride above all the ruckus, not letting any of it bother him.

Did I make the wrong decision inviting her? Kate now wished she hadn't. Sure, Melissa had come over and helped paint the fence, and she seemed genuinely sorry for the snobby way she'd treated them before. *Being nice for a day or two is one thing,* Kate thought. *But sometimes people don't change, even if you think they have.*

The last thing Kate wanted was to bring more trouble into her own life, much less Tori's or Colt's. They had enough to do with getting the Ferris family's horse barn up and running with paying customers.

Kate settled into the couch with a bowl of popcorn and grinned at her friends, excited they'd made the decision to come and talk about the parade. Her mom and dad had said they'd consider allowing them to ride in the parade after they heard what ideas Kate, Tori, Colt, and Melissa came up with, so at least they hadn't said no first thing.

Kate clicked the remote and turned off the TV. "That was a good movie, but we'd better get back to planning. Melissa, you're in charge, so you should take over."

Melissa's blonde curls bounced with excitement. "I've been thinking about it all day. First, we need to make banners to drape behind our saddles with the barn name. Second, we need to come up with colorful costumes we can wear, or our horses can wear—something that will draw attention. We could wear our riding outfits, but will anyone really notice us if we do? Isn't that too"—she made air quotes—"*normal?*"

Colt slumped back against the couch. "I hope you don't mean doing something dumb like dressing up as *Arabian Nights* or fairy-tale characters. That would not be cool. I don't see why I can't be a cowboy riding a horse. After all, it is a parade for the Fort Dalles Rodeo."

"I get your point, Colt," Tori added. "But Melissa might be right. Lots of people ride horses in parades—the rodeo princesses and clubs—and pretty soon you hardly notice them. Maybe we do need something a little different to stand out."

"But where would we get costumes, and how would we pay for them? And what kind of banners would we make?" Kate pondered a minute. "Paper would rip too easily, and I'm no good at sewing. I've seen horses with silk banners and professional lettering, but we can't afford that. It's a great idea, but we have to make sure that whatever we decide will work."

"I see what you mean," Melissa said. "Our regular riding gear would be cheap and easy, but do we really want to look cheap?" She tossed her head. "I sure don't."

Tori sighed and shot a glance at Kate. "Maybe we could think of a way to earn money for nice banners or costumes. I agree that we need something that catches people's attention."

Colt nodded. "That might work. If you girls want to do a bunch of baking, we could have a bake sale."

Kate raised her brows. "And what would the boy be doing while the girls are baking?"

Colt smirked. "Licking the bowl and doing quality control on the goodies."

Tori smacked his arm. "More like washing the dishes and doing publicity."

Melissa gazed from one to the other, her mouth agape. "Are you guys like this all the time?"

Kate snickered. "Pretty much. We can be serious when we have to be though." She probably should say she was sorry, but after Melissa's stuck-up comment about not looking cheap, the words would have choked her. Apparently some of the old Melissa was still hanging around. "Let's get back to business. Colt suggested a bake sale. What else?"

"A car wash?" Melissa offered.

"Or maybe some kind of raffle," Tori added.

Kate set her soda glass on the table. "That might work. I could talk to Mom about raffling off a riding lesson."

"But you'd have to pay the trainer for the lesson, right? Would it be worth it?" Melissa asked.

"If enough people bought a ticket, we'd raise more than the lesson cost. But it might not be the best prize. We probably need to think about that a little longer." Kate leaned against the couch.

Colt drummed his fingers on the coffee table. "Yeah. Having a good prize would get a lot more buyers."

At that moment Kate's attention was drawn to a slight figure in the doorway to the hall leading upstairs. Her little brother, Pete, stood there, clutching his blanket. He shuffled his feet toward her.

Kate jumped up. "Pete. Why aren't you in bed? Are you looking for Mom? She's in the TV room with Dad."

He didn't respond and kept his eyes averted.

She walked across the room. "What's the matter, little guy? Can't sleep again?"

He hunched one shoulder.

Kate knew better than to draw him into a hug like she wanted to do. Her six-year-old, autistic brother didn't like to be touched unless it was his idea. "Want me to take you back to your room and tuck you in?"

"Want a drink of water."

Melissa suddenly appeared at Pete's side and touched his brown hair, but he didn't pull back. "I can get it for you, buddy."

Kate glanced at the girl, then at her brother. It had amazed her the first time she'd seen this soft side of Melissa with her brother, and it still had the ability to surprise her. Not that she wasn't glad. Melissa could as easily have been mean to Pete. So many people didn't understand kids with problems. "Thanks, Melissa. But I'll take him."

Melissa gave a short nod. "Okay." She headed back to the couch and sank into the cushions.

"Pete?" Kate's mom stepped into the room. "There you are. Come on, honey, let's go." She extended her hand, and Pete moved to her side but didn't reach out to her. "You kids go ahead with your planning, and I'll get this little guy back to bed." She touched Pete on his back and urged him toward the hallway.

Kate called after them, "He wants water, Mom."

"I'll take care of it. Thanks, Kate." Mom disappeared around the corner.

Silence fell over the group. Then Melissa got up. "I'd better go. Mom said she'd be waiting outside at seven thirty, and it's twenty-five after now. Thanks for inviting me. I hope you have fun the rest of the night." She smirked slightly.

"Bye, Melissa," their voices chorused as Melissa headed out the door.

"Keep thinking of ideas," Kate called after her.

Colt grabbed the remote. "Want to watch a scary movie?"

Tori groaned. "I hate scary movies. They scare me."

"That's the idea, silly."

Kate elbowed him. "We don't even own any scary movies. What did you guys think about Melissa?"

Tori sobered. "What do you mean?"

"I don't know. She was helpful and everything, but she seemed ... odd somehow. I can't explain it."

Colt rolled his eyes. "You're imagining things, Kate. If anything, she's more normal than we are." He grinned.

Tori huffed. "Colt, sometimes I want to smack you."

He shrank away as though scared but grinned again, wider.

"Seriously, I didn't notice anything weird about her," Tori reasoned. "Except for the comment about not looking cheap, but that didn't really surprise me. Maybe she was worried she wouldn't fit in. We're not exactly the crowd she runs with, you know."

Kate thought for a moment. "Well it kinda bugged me. I guess it's still hard for me to believe she wants to be our friend, after the way she acted toward us for so long."

Colt kicked off his shoes, leaned into the couch, and planted his heels on the coffee table. "Ah, she's all right. I don't think she's a Christian, though. I guess it's up to us to do the right thing and make her feel welcome."

Kate hesitated. "I just don't want to get burned. Know what I mean?" Melissa seemed decent enough now, but was she only playing a game, maybe because she was bored? Would she then go back to her old self?

The other two were quiet, as if thinking.

Finally Tori announced, "But we should give her a chance, right?"

"Right," Colt said swiftly.

Kate chimed in with her agreement a bit more slowly. "I wonder what else she had to do tonight. A little late to be heading to another friend's house, and with school out, there's no homework."

Colt drew in a deep breath and blew it out, his eyes closing. "If you don't want to watch another movie, maybe I'll take a little nap."

Kate waved a hand in front of her face. "Remember what we said about your stinky socks? We weren't kidding!" She placed her foot next to his ankle and pushed. "Ugh. Boys are gross."

Colt sat up. "Aww! You've stuck a knife right through my heart." He chuckled. "I probably should head home too. Mind if I use your phone and give Mom a call?"

"Go ahead. You know where it is. You sure you don't want any more popcorn first?"

"Not me." The answers came in unison from Colt and Tori.

Colt's long stride took him out of the room in a couple of seconds, but he hollered over his shoulder, "Hey, come see this. Weird, if you ask me."

Kate bolted into the kitchen first, with Tori on her heels, and said, "What's up?"

Colt moved to the sliding-glass door and pointed. "A black horse. That's not a big deal, but the rider looks strange."

Tori crept up beside him. "The horse is gorgeous!"

Colt grunted assent. "But what's the deal with the person riding him? You can't tell if it's a man or a woman, and it's awful warm to be wearing a full slicker with a hood."

Kate shaded her eyes against the glass. "I wish it wasn't dusk, so we could see the rider better. Look, they're trotting now and moving on up the road. I think the rider's a woman or a teen-ager. Doesn't look big enough to be a man, and he's all hunched over the horse's mane. Do you think she's sick or something?"

Colt slid the door open. "Maybe we should make sure the rider is okay."

Kate and Tori slipped outside, with Colt following. He nudged Kate in the side. "You going to holler or just stand there?"

Kate made a face at him but took a few steps toward the gravel road that ran behind their house. "Hey," she called toward the horse and rider, "are you all right?"

The horse slowed for a second. Then the rider bumped him in the side and took off at a fast trot.

Tori stepped up beside Kate. "That was rude. She had to have heard you, but then she ignored you."

Kate nodded. "It's a mystery. I've never seen that horse before, but maybe we should ask around and see what we can find out. It sure seemed like the rider had something to hide." She faced Tori and Colt. "The person was the same size as Melissa. You don't suppose that's why she had to hurry home? But why wouldn't she stop and show us her new horse?"

Colt scrunched his brow. "It doesn't make a bit of sense. I say we keep a close eye out tomorrow night in case the rider comes back. What if she stole that horse?"

Books by Miralee Ferrell

Horses and Friends Series
A Horse for Kate
Silver Spurs

Love Blossoms in Oregon Series
Blowing on Dandelions
Forget Me Not
Wishing on Buttercups
Dreaming on Daisies

The 12 Brides of Christmas Series
The Nativity Bride

Love Finds You Series
Love Finds You in Bridal Veil, Oregon
Love Finds You in Sundance, Wyoming
Love Finds You in Last Chance, California
Love Finds You in Tombstone, Arizona
(sequel to *Love Finds You in Last Chance, California*)
The Other Daughter
Finding Jeena
(sequel to *The Other Daughter*)

Other Contributions/Compilations
A Cup of Comfort for Cat Lovers
Fighting Fear: Winning the War at Home
Faith & Finances: In God We Trust
Faith & Family: A Christian Living Daily
Devotional for Parents and Their Kids

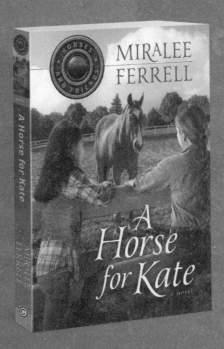

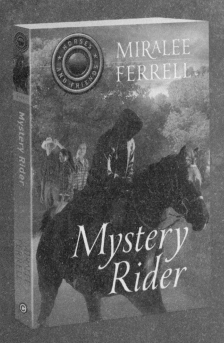